I0552927

Surviving
SYDNEY

Surviving SYDNEY

A WICKED TAILS STORY

SHELBY KENT-STEWART

honeysuckle house

Published by Honeysuckle Houses, Charleston, SC

Paperback ISBN: 978-0-9910425-7-9
eBook ISBN: 978-0-9910425-8-6

For Bob

All the proof I need that superheroes exist.

1

Activity in the foreground, diffused light and smoke. The screen goes dark as speakers blast the first few notes of Benny and the Jets. Moments later, a beam lights a platform. At its center is a pole, a figure draped around it, her back to the camera. She is nude, lithe, erotically female. Platinum hair grazes porcelain shoulders and catches the light as she sways. Her back slopes, dips and flares. A heart-shaped ass tops well-toned legs and four-inch stilettos, shoulder-width apart. Seducing the pole, she squats, her movements fluid, more languid than lewd. She rises, turns and chaos ensues. Her breasts are firm, nipples rosy and erect, mound waxed smooth and littered with rhinestones. Elton would be proud. As she swings her head, her face is revealed and...

"Holy. Shit." I gaped at the computer screen. In the last twenty years, I'd viewed hundreds of surveillance tapes. Most bored me to tears, a few made me puke and some made me laugh. But never *ever* had one left me with a hard-on.

Dylan Hunt, my business partner, hit the pause button and Sydney Forrest's eyes froze on mine. They were beautiful eyes, large and expressive. When she was angry, they went from cornflower to cobalt in the length of a heartbeat. Not that I'd noticed. And I'd bet next year's salary, the same thing would happen when she climaxed. Not that I cared.

Leaning back in his chair, Dylan laced his fingers behind his head and nodded to the laptop. "The disc came in three days ago by regular mail addressed to both of us, no note and no return address. Judging from the angle and movement, it's not a security camera. I'm guessing it was shot with a pretty decent hand-held job. I Googled the name on the sign behind her. *Naughty Nellie's* is a strip joint off Broadway in San Francisco. In the past year, four strippers from that club have gone missing. So far, they've identified three of the four from body parts found scattered around the city."

"Christ." The video was disturbing enough. The last thing I needed were the images of butchered women imprinted on my brain. As much as I loathed the freaking Middle East, I was beginning to wish I'd stayed there.

"A couple of days ago, I talked to a detective Greer with the SFPD. They've got squat on the perp but he gave me a description of the victims, mid to late twenties, slender, petite and blonde."

"That explains the wig. Does she know we have this?"

"Nope. Since you were coming back anyway, I figured I'd wait for you. Level with me, J.D., did it ever occur to you that she was hiding that body under those cargo pants and lab coat?"

Rhetorical or not, the question pissed me off. At the moment, the only part of her anatomy I wanted my hands on was her silky white neck. "What's your point?"

"No point. I just find it curious that three weeks after we hired her you pulled Jared out of Bahrain on some cockamamie pretense, took his place and hid out there for two months."

"In the first place, Dr. Phil, I wasn't hiding out, I was working. And in the second, third and fourth places, she's an employee, her old man is Deputy Director of the CIA and she's gay. Where I come from, that's called three strikes, you're out."

Dylan grinned. "She's also gorgeous, smart as a whip and glues rhinestones to her pussy. Where I come from, we fall to our knees and praise Jesus."

"Where you come from, a virgin is an eight-year-old who can outrun her brothers."

Okay, I admit it, I was cranky. There was a time when I could cross multiple time zones, jump from a plane and raise hell for a week without sleep. But now that I was pushing

3

forty, jet lag was more reality than theory, and after twenty hours in the air, I was ready for some serious rack time. What I wasn't prepared for was being pulled kicking and screaming into Dr. Sydney Forrest's psyche. That was Dylan's job. "Tell you what, you deal with her and I'll go home, grab a shower and some shuteye."

He got that look, the one he got right before he laid some psychobabble mumbo jumbo on me, the one where he used reason and logic to talk me off the ledge. That look was bad enough on a grown man but I'd seen it since we were kids and it creeped me out.

"Look, J.D., I know you're tired and you look like shit, but there's a reason I waited for you. She works for both of us and we need to put up a united front here. Since I've seen her every day and established a working relationship with her, let me do the talking."

"What am I supposed to do, stand here and growl at her?"

"You have to admit, no one does it better. You're the wild card, amigo. Before you ran out of here like your ass was on fire, I saw the way she responded to you and you scared the shit out of her. She couldn't even look you in the eye. The fact that you've been gone works to our advantage. No one but me knew you were coming back today. She'll think you came back because of the disc."

"You're an evil sonofabitch, you know that?"

"But you missed me, didn't you?"

And just like that, he turned from Dr. Death to Opie Taylor. It's one of the things I like best about him, one of the reasons we've been friends for thirty years; that and the fact that we have very different taste in women. He likes them tall, mean and dumb as a doorknob. I don't.

"We need some answers, J.D."

His comment about her not being able to look me in the eye bothered me more than it should have, more than I cared to admit, but he was right about needing answers. Something wasn't right. I got up and began to pace. "We know she went to S. F. and managed to wangle a job at the titty bar, that she fit the description of the four missing women closely enough to where she only had to change her hair. I think we can safely assume she was either using herself as bait or she figured it was the easiest way to gather evidence and information the cops might have missed."

"Which means she's in breach of her contract here," said Dylan.

"Fair enough and we'll deal with it but that still doesn't explain the tape."

"It would if she wanted out of her contract. Think about it. While she's playing Nancy Drew, she had someone accompany her to San Francisco and shoot the video. She sent it to us, assuming we'd have no choice but to release her. She's a brilliant scientist and I'm sure there are any number of labs around the country that would snap her up. Maybe she got a better offer. Maybe her girlfriend doesn't like the fact that she's the only woman here under seventy and she's surrounded by testosterone all day. We know the Feds grabbed her right out of grad school and she lasted less than a year. Maybe she's the type who needs a challenge every few months. With the lab almost finished, maybe she's bored. Who the hell knows?"

Typical of Dylan, he'd thought everything through and tied it up in a nice, neat package and I bought it, every well-reasoned word. The only other possible explanation was the stuff of bad fiction writers. *Beautiful forensic scientist goes undercover to catch a serial killer but someone is stalking her. Is it the killer? Or is it a warning from some faceless foe that the organization for which she works is penetrable, that their alliances and secrets are vulnerable? If they can get to her, is everyone at risk? Will International Investigations and Facilitations go the way of the dodo bird?*

Bullshit. I bought Dylan's theory because it made sense and because I felt vindicated. I'd been against bringing her in from the beginning and was obnoxiously vocal in my objections: her father was a spook, she came from money, she was spoiled, she was young and she was female. Shamelessly, I pulled out all the stops. The only thing I didn't throw into the mix was her sexual preference. I was an asshole and a hypocrite but no one would ever accuse me of being a homophobe.

When push came to shove, I folded. After ten years, our reputation and client list were golden and we needed to expand. We needed a state-of-the-art forensics lab and a state-of-the-art scientist to pull it together. And we needed it now.

Sydney Forrest fit the bill like a glove. With a Joint Doctorate in Forensic and Behavioral Sciences and a year with the FBI, she was poised, professional and eager. Her references were impeccable. Everyone loved her and those who didn't respected her. She was perfect for the job. Dylan was ecstatic, I was sullen and Sydney was hired.

And now she was about to be fired.

2

Life is an adventure in forgiveness.
—Norman Cousins

"Sydney, snap out of it and talk to me. Who was on the phone? You're scaring me."

Amanda's voice pierced the fog in my brain and I shook my head to clear it. As I turned to look at her, I caught my reflection in the mirror. No wonder she was scared. My eyes were twice their normal size, my skin a deadly shade of pale and my hair? Well, my hair looked pretty much the way it always did, a mess.

"Sydney!"

I reached for her hand and squeezed it. "That was Detective Greer. It was him, Mandy. They picked up the bastard last night and he confessed. He also confessed to murdering the fourth woman, Marina Ivanov, and told them where he disposed of her body."

"Oh my God, Syd, that's incredible. You're incredible. I'm so proud of you." She hugged me and pulled back to grip my forearms. "They're not using your name, are they? You deserve the credit and all but. . ."

"Believe me, the last thing I want is credit and Greer assured me if they referred to me at all, it would be as an unnamed source. The police want me out of the picture as much as I want to stay out. If Hunt finds out about this, I'll be toast." *And Jordan Dunham will do the happy dance all the way back from Bahrain.*

"But what if the creep decides to lawyer-up and recant? Won't that mean a trial and won't you have to . . .?"

"Breathe, Mandy. Everything's going to be fine." But even as I said the words, I knew there was an outside chance that things could play out exactly as Amanda feared and the prosecution would have no choice but to put me on the stand. And if that happened, a clever defense attorney would have me for lunch.

"Just so we're clear, Dr. Forrest, let's see if we have all the facts, shall we? Knowing full well that you were in violation of your contract with International Investigations and Facilitations, you deceived your employers, drove two hundred and twenty-five miles from your home in Atascadero and lied your way into a job at Naughty Nellie's by misrepresenting yourself as an exotic dancer.

You did this because you had deduced from afar that, because the four unfortunate women were all eastern European, the perpetrator would share that characteristic and you wanted to view the audience from their vantage point. On the fifth and last night of your (he pauses to clear his throat) performance, you felt a change in the energy of the room. You looked out and, lo and behold, you saw a swarthy man staring at you. At that point, you decided to entrap him by executing a particularly lascivious dance move directed at him and when he returned your advances with a glare, you were convinced you had your man. But instead of alerting the police, who actually have jurisdiction in our fair city, you took it upon yourself to taint the forensic evidence by surreptitiously collecting his glass and mailing it to Detective Greer in a shoebox. Flash forward a week later and, wonder of wonders, the defendant's thumbprint matches that of a partial print found on a necklace belonging to one of the victims. I suppose my only question for you, Dr. Forrest, is why we didn't use you to sniff out Osama Bin Laden."

Deceived. Lied. Entrapped. Tainted. The tactic was as old as jurisprudence. Denigrate the witness and mitigate the crime. Still, I had little doubt in the end justice would be served. As for me, if the worst came to pass and the case went to trial, I would kiss my career good-bye. All things considered, I could live with that.

But for the foreseeable future I had a career and a job, and if I didn't move my butt, I'd be late. Introspection could wait. It was a day for celebration, a day to put the top down on my aging Fiat Spider, let my hair blow free and sing along with *Adele*. It was the best of all possible days, the day I learned I'd made a difference.

To the outside world, IIF was a run-of-the-mill security company, our building singularly unimpressive, intentionally so. Tucked away in an industrial park abutting Paso Robles Airport, it was one ugly building among many, the type you wouldn't look at twice, the kind you'd never suspect housed some of the most sophisticated technology available. And in less than a week - drum roll please - it would also house a first-class forensics lab.

Put simply, Dunham and Hunt were the go-to guys and we, the thirty or so people who worked for them, were the ones the go-to guys relied on to investigate and facilitate. We were the *Ghostbusters* of International diplomacy, the first and best defense against embarrassment, banishment and all hell breaking loose.

If a prominent Swiss banking family suspected that one of their own was dipping in the till but didn't want to involve the Swiss authorities, *who ya gonna call*? If the head of Al-Mukhabarat al-'Ammah, Egypt's General Intelligence Directorate, was leaving more state secrets than semen in his mistress's bed, *who ya gonna call*? If the Ambassador from the United Arab Emirates was getting his kicks on Route 66 with a conservative red state senator, well, you get the picture.

I wasn't naïve. I knew things like this went on everyday

but the frequency with which they happened kept us hopping. We were up to our collective asses in nefarious activities, our resources stretched to the max.

I loved my job. IIF was where I was happiest. It felt like home, a big noisy home with thirty brothers who coddled me, made me laugh and teased me unmercifully. The year I spent at Quantico was hell but this was different. Then again, I was different, different by design.

If we were the worker bees, Grace was the Queen. She watched over all of us but particularly Hunt and Dunham, whose offices she guarded like a British bulldog. Old enough to know better and too old to care, she was still a beautiful woman, regal, with a wicked sense of humor. During her forty-odd years with MI6, she'd seen and done it all and stayed single in the process. Rumors abounded about her colorful past, including one that hinted she was Ian Fleming's inspiration for *Moneypenny*, the sexy secretary who found her way into James Bond's heart if not his bed, a rumor she would neither confirm nor deny.

And last but not least, there was Dylan Hunt and Jordan Dunham, my bosses, for whom the term *study in contrasts* was invented. I liked Dr. Hunt immensely. With his blond good looks and ready smile, he put me instantly at ease. Smart, funny and supportive, he made me feel part of the team and I was grateful, more grateful than he knew.

Jordan Dunham, J.D. to all but me, was the Prince of

Darkness. Approximately the same impressive height and build as Hunt, Dunham's body gave off a dangerous vibe, carnal and cunning. Where Hunt's muscular build was camouflaged by chinos and button-downs, Dunham preferred jeans and t-shirts or turtlenecks, the tighter the better. Instead of walking, he swaggered; instead of talking, he barked. And his face? It was the face of a superhero, one I could easily imagine gracing the front of a comic book. All lines and planes, his features were chiseled, his jaw accentuated by a chinstrap beard and goatee, black as coal, the same as his hair. His eyes were deep, fathomless pits of chocolate and above them two perfectly-shaped eyebrows, one of which he tended to arch frequently and effectively in my direction. He scared the crap out of me, among other things, so it was with no small amount of relief that three weeks after I was hired, I learned he had boogied out of Dodge and flown straight to Bahrain. Maybe if I were really, really lucky, he'd stay there.

My car shimmied to a stop and I was inside the lab in less than a minute. I felt another wave of happiness, my second for the day, a personal best. The lab was shaping up to be everything I'd hoped and I'd done it ahead of schedule and within my allocated budget. It was my baby.

Knowing full well that pride goeth before a fall, I was still somewhat surprised when Grace summoned me to Dylan's office. When I got there, the doors to both his and Jordan's offices were closed.

Just outside, Grace motioned me to sit. "They'll be just a moment, dear."

"They?"

"J.D. flew in early this morning."

My smile vanished and I fought the urge to bolt. I must have zoned for a second and when I came to my senses, Grace was looking at me strangely.

"I'm sorry, Grace. Did you say something?"

"I asked if you could pout, dear."

Pout? And then it hit me. I was in trouble. "I don't think I can do that."

"Don't be ridiculous, Sydney. Every woman can do that. The instructions were included in your first box of tampons. Inside that office, you're at DEFCON 2 which requires pouting at the very least. If things reach DEFCON 1, be prepared to shed tears."

I was still giggling when Dylan's door opened and Jordan's presence filled the space. "Something funny you'd like to share, Dr. Forrest?"

The first words out of his mouth confirmed Grace's threat assessment. Everyone knew I hated the title and rarely used it. Demonstrating more bravado than I felt at the moment, I squared my shoulders and made eye contact. "Welcome back, Jordan. How was Bahrain?"

One eyebrow lifted a fraction of an inch and the corner of his mouth twitched. "Hot."

Thus concluded the entertainment portion of our program. A minute later, I was sitting in front of Dylan's desk and Jordan was holding up a wall, arms folded over his expansive chest, long legs crossed at the ankles.

Whatever this was about, I had no intention of cowering like a schoolgirl. "Is there a problem?"

Dylan leaned forward, his face absent its normally pleasant expression. "Sydney, you're an intelligent woman, so we assume you actually read your employment contract before you signed it."

"Of course I read it but I don't…"

"Don't what, think it applies to you? The reason we're insistent that our employees keep us apprised of their travel plans outside a hundred mile radius is to ensure their safety. For every client, there's some person or persons who wants to make political hay of the situation. There are also people who would have no qualms about detaining one of our people in exchange for information on our operation and client list. We also pay our employees extremely well so they're not forced to take outside jobs."

Political hay? The longer he talked, the more confused I became. "You think I'm moonlighting?"

"Fuck it."

I jumped at Jordan's invective and watched as he pushed away from the wall and leaned over Dylan's desk. The next sound I heard rendered me paralyzed and mute. *Benny and the*

Jets. A glance at the laptop made my heart stop.

Closing my eyes, I dropped my head. It was the only way I could process my emotions. Was I angry, hurt, embarrassed? I felt all those things, but in the end resignation won out as always. I'd taken a calculated risk and lost. I wanted to crawl into a hole and cry but I would have gouged out my eyes before I shed a tear in front of these men.

"Please turn it off." When Dylan did as I asked, I lifted my head and looked at them. "I didn't keep the money. I divided it up among the other girls."

"Sydney, if you wanted out of your contract, why didn't you simply come and talk to us?" The edge was gone from Dylan's voice but I actually preferred it to the one he was using now, the patronizing psychiatrist's voice.

"I don't want out of my contract. I love my job. I had no idea you were having me followed. Why did you do that?"

Two new sounds assailed me at once. Jordan snorted and Dylan clucked. "Sydney, please."

"Please what?"

Jordan had moved back against the wall and was studying me. It was a look I hadn't seen before, not on him. Kindness? Tenderness? Whatever it was, it made me feel vulnerable and achy. I was sure my cheeks were burning red.

And just as quickly, his expression changed. He was back to being my inquisitor, my Prince of Darkness. "First things first. We know about the murdered women, Sydney. What we don't know is why you made yourself a target. What's your interest in the case?"

It would have been easy to bare my soul and let them peek into my heart, to share my success and beg them for another chance. But I could do none of those things without betraying an elemental part of who I was and that I wouldn't do. I wouldn't beg, never again. It was a promise I'd made to a lost little girl, a girl who looked a lot like me. Knowing my response would seal my fate, I was past caring. "That's none of your business. Just tell me how many copies of the disc are floating around out there."

"You tell us."

I was so far down the rabbit hole, I feared I'd never climb out. "Wait. You think I had someone film me? You think I sent you the disc? Is that what you meant about me trying to get out of my contract? You can't be serious. I'm mortified." I looked directly at Jordan. For whatever reason, I wanted him to believe me.

Nodding at the laptop, he arched an eyebrow. "Funny, you don't look mortified, chilly maybe, but hardly mortified."

Bastard. I had just enough strength to finish this. "If you'll have someone escort me back to the lab, I'll get my things and leave."

Dylan rose from behind his desk and came toward me. "That's not necessary, Sydney. We trust that you aren't going to steal anything."

"It's protocol, Dr. Hunt, and as much for my protection as yours. Since you both have such a low opinion of me already, it's hardly a leap to think you would accuse me of theft." Before he could comment, I added, "Last night, I wrote up a status report on the lab and prepared a punch list of the equipment we're still waiting for. I'll email it to you later today. Until you find my replacement, Scotty can handle the day-to-day."

As I left his office, I looked for Grace but she wasn't at her desk. It was just as well. Chances are I would have broken down and since Jordan was right behind me, the last thing I wanted was a scene. Skirting the bullpen to avoid as many people as possible, I took the back way to the lab.

Jordan stuck to me like glue, a constant reminder that my day had taken an unexpected turn, and with it my future. Gone were my plans for putting down roots on California's Central Coast and buying a small house in Templeton so I'd be closer to work. I was back to square one, adrift.

Exhausted and emotionally frayed, I looked around the lab and saw pieces of myself, an extra pair of boots, two shelves of books, a plant or two. I couldn't do this, not today, not with the Prince of Darkness hovering, watching my every move, waiting for me to break.

Taking a breath, I turned and looked up at him. "I'd like to come back tomorrow morning and say good-bye to everyone. I'll bring some boxes and pack up my books then. Is that all right?"

"Was it worth it, Sydney?"

If his voice was cold, his eyes were like ice. I knew he was talking about the disc but I didn't care how they got it. Perhaps I should have, but I didn't. For all I knew, it was a set-up. Jordan wanted me gone and had me tailed, hoping for an indiscretion. Instead, I focused on the four dead women and the man behind bars, the one I'd helped put there, the one who would never take another life. Stepping back so I could look him in the eye, I smiled. "Absolutely."

His eyes narrowed and his body tensed.

"Tell me the truth, Jordan, now that I'm leaving anyway. I know you interviewed several candidates for my job, all of whom you preferred over me. Why is that? Why didn't you want me?"

He didn't miss a beat. It was as if he'd rehearsed the speech a million times. "I have a problem with spoiled little rich girls who breeze through life, thinking they can get away with anything because they have daddy to fall back on. You were with the Bureau what, a year? What happened, did you get bored or did the Forrest name not buy you enough preferential treatment? I knew you were trouble the minute I laid eyes on you and this last escapade just confirmed it. You're a loose cannon, Sydney, and loose cannons are dangerous."

His words cut deep and drew blood. I didn't know which hurt worst, seeing the scorn on his face or learning that he wasn't a superhero after all. He was just another man who used words instead of weapons.

And then I did the strangest thing. Right before I grabbed my tote bag and ran for my car, I reached up, touched his cheek and whispered, "I'm sorry."

I wonder why I did that.

3

I was in Hell which, upon reflection, was exactly where I belonged. No matter what I did, sleep eluded me. Every time I closed my eyes, I heard her speak my name or felt her fingers on my skin. The worst moments were when I saw her face, the way her eyes filled when she looked up at me and asked, *"Why didn't you want me?"*

Want her? Hell, yes, I wanted her. From that first interview, there was rarely a moment when I didn't think about her, the way that tangle of copper hair would look in my bed, the way her lips — Sweet Jesus what lips — would feel around my cock. I wanted to lick every inch of her alabaster skin starting with the freckles on her nose, that tiny nose that scrunched up when she was puzzled. And when I licked my way to her pussy, I wanted her to come so hard that her cream would fill my mouth. And yeah, I wanted to take her to The Trident and show her off, dress her in some sexy little number and tie her up, tie her down and tie her to me forever.

The lust I could deal with but it was the other thing that had my gut in knots, the thing I travelled half a world away to escape. I wanted to cherish and protect her, lock her in a castle and raise the drawbridge. I wanted to slay the dragons and kill the demons I saw lurking in her eyes. I wanted her in every way a man wants a woman and in ways no woman should be wanted. You bet your ass I wanted her, and because I couldn't have her, I hurt her.

With all the finesse of a baby rattler, I went straight for her throat and injected my venom. Did I believe the things I said to her? Yes and no, not that I gave a shit. I'd chosen my words to inflict the most amount of pain, to incite her to do exactly what she did, run. And what would I do when she came back for her things? Apologize? Grovel? Not even close. I planned to hide out in my office. I was a coward but I wasn't fucking stupid.

I'd also been around long enough to believe the adage *when it rains, it pours*, so when I saw the official looking vehicle in the parking lot, I was tempted to reach for an umbrella. In hindsight, I should have reached for my gun.

Roger Forrest, Deputy Director of the CIA, was waiting for

me in my office and Grace wasn't happy. In fact, she appeared downright surly, not a good look for a woman nearing eighty. The door was closed and he couldn't hear us but she crooked her finger at me anyway and made me lean in so she could whisper, "Remind me to fumigate your office when he leaves, J.D. I've heard hydrogen cyanide works nicely."

Because of her years with MI6, Grace made no bones about her disdain for the CIA, but I also knew she was fond of Sydney and disapproved of the way we'd handled her termination. Hoping for the best, I whispered back, "You want me in or out of my office when you release the cyanide?"

That made her smile. "Inside would be lovely, dear."

It was going to be a long fucking day.

Forrest was a big S.O.B., linebacker big. I'm six-four and we stood eye to eye; but he outweighed me by fifty pounds, the bulk of which had settled in his gut. I'm sure at one time he'd been a good-looking man but those days were gone. Having your ass kissed daily is all well and good but it doesn't afford much opportunity for exercise.

We shook hands, sniffed each other's butts and then we both sat down. It didn't take a genius to figure out why he'd come. The little princess had called daddy and he was there to plead her case. Knowing how much a guy like him got off on power, I sat back to hear his pitch. This was going to be fun.

"To what do I owe the honor of a visit from the Deputy Director of the CIA?" No sooner had the words left my mouth than I regretted them. The office was big enough for only one pompous prick and I'd already tagged him as *it*.

"I'm not here in an official capacity, Mr. Dunham. I'm here as a father. I want you to release my daughter from her contract."

"Excuse me?"

"I assume there's some kind of formal agreement between yourselves and your employees."

"There is."

"I thought as much. Name your price. If you won't do it at the behest of a concerned father, then perhaps you'll allow me to buy her out of her contract."

"Look, Forrest . . ."

He didn't like that. He was accustomed to being handled with deference and I'd just kicked him in the nuts.

He smiled a nasty little smile and raised his hand. "Let me make something clear to you, Dunham. I know all about you, your partner and this organization and I can have you closed down within the hour. I came here as a reasonable man with a reasonable request but we can play this either way."

The thing about two-word responses is that it drives the other guy nuts. His goal is to have you shaking in your boots. Your goal is to keep him talking so he'll spit out whatever's in his craw, leave and you can lock your door and take a nap. If you can manage a yawn or two, so much the better. "Do tell."

"I know that you and Dylan Hunt were brought up on

neighboring vineyards here in Paso Robles and that you were in your second year at Cal Poly when you married your high school sweetheart but left in your third year to join the military when she ran off with one of her professors. I know you were in Special Forces and saw action in Somalia in '93 and Kosovo in '99, after which you left the military with an exemplary service record.

"Hunt chose a different path. While you were trying to avoid getting your ass shot off or worse, he attended eight years of medical school and started a lucrative psychiatric practice in nearby San Luis Obispo.

"In 2001, you joined forces and launched International Investigations and Facilitations. Essentially, you are high-end private investigators who solve problems for the rich and powerful, some of whom represent governments around the world. I also know you walk a fine line between ethics and espionage."

I was bored. "As the number two man in what is arguably the most formidable intelligence agency in the world, I'm neither impressed nor intimidated by the fact that you know who we are, Forrest."

"Arguably the most formidable? You have doubts?"

"Not me. I know for a fact that the CIA is a cluster-fuck and American intelligence is an oxymoron. Even my five-year-old nephew has figured that one out."

"Yes, well, you're entitled to your opinion, until such time as it affects my standing and reputation in the grand scheme of things."

"Meaning?"

He seemed to be mulling over how much he wanted to divulge but he must have decided to go for broke and lay his cards on the table. "I plan to make a run for the Senate from my home state of Connecticut. The scrutiny on my family will be intense and I have no intention of allowing an opponent to publish photographs of my only child with her tits hanging out and her..."

"Stop!" That shut him up which was a good thing. If he'd said another word, I was prepared to leap across the desk, rip his balls off and shove them down his throat. Then maybe I could get my nap.

As a trained investigator, I was accustomed to expecting the unexpected and connecting the dots, but his next statement knocked me on my ass.

"I assume you got the disc."

"You sent the disc?"

"An associate of mine filmed her outrageous stunt and sent it to you under my instructions."

"And Sydney knew nothing about it?"

"Contrary to your earlier statements, we're very good at what we do, Dunham. She had no idea she was being followed and filmed."

I swallowed a groan and tried to regroup. "Let's stop with

the bullshit and explain to me why you're here instead of having this discussion with Sydney."

"Very well. My daughter is headstrong with a mind of her own and we rarely see eye to eye. When I discovered she was working for you, I wasn't thrilled about it but I assumed her activities would be contained and limited to the work for which she was trained. When I made the decision to enter the political arena, I thought it best to have someone monitor those activities to ensure that her life hadn't taken a turn that would jeopardize my decision. Imagine my chagrin when I learned you had chosen to exploit her obvious physical attributes in what I can only assume was some kind of undercover operation. The only other plausible explanation is that she's lost her mind and should be committed. Frankly, I don't care either way. I want her out of this organization and ensconced in a teaching post which I've secured for her closer to home."

"You're a real piece of work, you know that?"

"Rest assured I will do whatever it takes to achieve my goals, Dunham, including invoking the Patriot Act to have you and Hunt rendered to the most disagreeable spot on the planet. Having said that, I would prefer to take the more civilized approach and simply buy your cooperation, so how much will it take?"

I was wrong. This wasn't fun at all. "Sydney's not for sale."

His shoulders deflated, but I had to hand it to him, he came back with a zinger. "Then you must be fucking her. Or perhaps you and Hunt are both fucking her. In that case, I'll add another zero."

Beneath the desk, my hands curled into fists and I counted to ten. When I commenced the smack-down, I wanted my thoughts as lucid as possible. "One. While I'm flattered you think Sydney would be interested in either of us, your comments reek of disrespect toward her and that doesn't sit well with me. Two. The next time you throw your considerable weight around and threaten someone, you'd better be damned sure your friends are higher up on the food chain than their friends. Yours aren't. Trust me on that. Three. The problem with arrogant assholes like you is that you think you're smarter than everyone else. You're not. This entire meeting has been taped, and if you ever show your face on our property again or attempt anything sleazy, it will be my pleasure to send copies to the *Washington Post*, *The New York Times*, CNN and I might even throw in the *National Enquirer* just for giggles. Four. Tell the goon you brought with you, the one who's been lurking behind the trees out there, that if he drops another cigarette butt on the ground, I'll make him pick every last one of them up with his teeth. Five. Your daughter has a name, it's Sydney. She's twenty-nine years old and obviously intelligent if she rarely sees eye to eye with you so stay the fuck out of her life. Are we done here?"

I watched his face go from red to purple and back to white.

It wasn't pretty but at least I'd gotten his attention. His eyes darted around the room, looking for the camera, but he never said another word, just picked himself up and walked out of my office.

My adrenalin was pumping when the connecting door to Dylan's office opened and he walked through it, collapsing in the chair Forrest had vacated. "What the fuck. What kind of father talks about his daughter like that?"

"Did you hear it all?"

"I heard it. You went easy on him. I would have kicked his ass all the way back to D.C."

"I came close when he brought up the disc. She was telling the truth." I caught something in Dylan's expression that suggested I was about to eat the cherry on the cake of my day. "What?"

He ran his hand over his face. "I was on-line a few minutes before he came in. A breaking news story caught my attention. They got the animal who murdered those women in San Francisco."

Not for one damn minute did I like the direction this conversation was heading. "Don't tell me."

"The details were sketchy so I called Greer. She nailed him, J.D. She got up on that stage, shook her sexy little booty and zeroed in on the bastard like a heat-seeking missile. She even retrieved the glass he was drinking from and sent it over to Greer. It matched a latent taken from one of the girls. They picked him up the night before last and he copped to all four murders."

Was it worth it, Sydney? Absolutely. "She knew it yesterday when we canned her."

"Then why the hell didn't she say something?"

"You're the shrink, you tell me. Maybe she thought our heads were so far up our asses we wouldn't hear her. Christ, I was brutal to her when I followed her into the lab and she never even tried to defend herself. She just looked up at me with those puppy dog eyes of hers."

What I didn't say, what I didn't want to look at, was how wrong I'd been on every point of my attack. Regardless of my reasons, I was no better than her father and that made me sick. No wonder she preferred pussy to cock.

Raised voices from the parking lot grabbed our attention. I looked at Dylan, Dylan looked at me and we both strode to the window. About fifty feet from where we were standing, Roger Forrest had Sydney by the arm and was pulling her toward the town car. Struggling to get away, she was pleading with him, her face streaked with tears. As we stood there gawking, preparing to turn on our heels and join the fray, several things happened at once.

Out of the corner of my eye, I spied Grace stomping across the parking lot with the same pissed-off expression I'd seen earlier. Only this time she was packing, and from what I could see, it was a 9 mm Glock. I had barely enough time to register that bit of bad news when the moron from the trees approached Sydney from behind, his intent clear, to push her into the car. Sensing him behind her, Sydney extricated herself at the very last second and executed a flawless roundhouse kick that connected her heel to his balls and his knees to the blacktop. Enraged, Forrest backhanded her across the face.

That's all we saw. By the time we reached the parking lot, Dickhead and Smoke Boy were burning rubber, Sydney was walking to her Fiat and Dirty Harry was aiming for the rear window of the fleeing car.

After I took the Glock from Grace, the three of us watched in silence as Sydney started her car. I didn't know what to do first, go after the bastard and lynch him from the nearest tree or run to her, pluck her out of the car and wrap her in my arms. While the former sounded good, the latter sounded better and I might have done it if Grace hadn't read my mind.

"She needs some space, J.D. You've done enough, both of you."

She turned around and walked back to the building, leaving Dylan and me standing there like idiots. A seventy-eight-year-old woman and a five-foot-four scientist had just taken out two men at least four times their weight and we hadn't broken a sweat.

Dylan shook his head. "I don't know about you but I'm

going to need serious therapy after this."

Under any other circumstances, I would have laughed but the pain in my gut was back with a vengeance. I'd fallen for someone who would never love me back. And that sucked. Big time.

4

If you haven't forgiven yourself something,
how can you forgive others?
— Dolores Huerta, Activist

They weren't the worst two days of my life. I'd had worse, much worse, days so dark that the shadows they cast would haunt me forever.

The confrontation with my father was not the first nor would it be the last. We were warriors in a battle that had raged throughout my life, the rules of engagement laid down when I was born. In exchange for his love, for a piece of his heart, I would sacrifice myself. Not literally, of course, although I sometimes wondered if even my death would put an end to our conflict. I could imagine him graveside, railing not at God but at me, cursing me for having the effrontery to leave him.

Bitch. Cunt. Whore. Those were the last words he hurled at me as he struck me, the words overheard by those who witnessed our skirmish. Not surprisingly, the pity on their faces cut deeper than his wrath. I was accustomed to his fury. It was all I'd ever known. While other children were lulled to sleep by nursery rhymes and love, I was schooled in the meaning of despair.

What saddened me at the moment had nothing to do with my father. It had everything to do with my pride. I should have held my head high and said my good-byes, but I didn't. Knowing I could never go back, not even for my books, I took the coward's path and fled.

Nor could I go home, not yet. The risk that he was there, laying in wait, was too great. Mandy could handle herself but the less she knew the better. If I kept her in the dark, she wouldn't have to lie. She was a terrible liar and her hatred for my father ran deep. I understood her feelings. Since college, she was the one who had witnessed the brutality of our combat, the one who supervised the triage on my soul.

No, I couldn't go home but I could visit Theresa, the only other person who wouldn't judge me, one of the few who understood.

It was comforting to be with her. The first time I came, I was stunned by the beauty and magic surrounding her, so much so that I researched it. What I learned made me smile. I learned that she was in the middle of the largest stand of

Monterey Pines in the state of California, that there were twelve hundred trees on the grounds, species ranging from the Monterey Pines to coastal live oaks, Toyons and California Pepper trees. And everywhere, with every breath, the sound of wind chimes tinkling on the breeze.

We'd never met, Theresa and me, but I knew her as well as I knew myself. During her life, she'd held nothing back, her books a testament to her courage. Those books gave me hope. Her death changed my life.

She was young when she died, thirty-five, the victim of a serial killer. I was twenty-two, bound for law school, my father's choice not mine. It was through her courage that I found my own and hatched my first rebellion.

Seven years later, when the opportunity presented itself at IIF, I took it as a sign. What were the odds that I would be spirited across the country to a job so close to where my mentor had lived her life and died?

So there I sat, staring at her gravestone, tracing the etching with my finger, a hummingbird, the name of her first book. Out of deference to her, I had taken that sweet creature as my totem. I wondered if she knew that around my neck I wore a locket, the tiny bird engraved on the front. I'd found it in an antique store in London and bought it on the spot. That same night, right before sleep, I wrote some words on a small piece of paper and enclosed them in the locket. They were her words, words that soothed me, words that reassured me I wasn't alone.

The wind kicked up and with it the music of the wind chimes. It was time to go, time to put my fears aside and plan my future.

I knew then that I was saying good-bye to her, that the next few weeks would be filled with activity and turmoil as I left one life and stepped into another. I wondered if she'd miss me.

In the meantime, I had one more spot to visit, one final farewell. I could sit there for hours, listen to the surf and dream about a life I'd never have.

No, they weren't the worst two days of my life. But they came close.

5

With any hope of a nap down the crapper, I got Sydney's home address off the computer and grabbed my car keys. If there was even a remote chance that the Dickhead would follow her home, he'd have to go through me. As far as the whole *space* thing, I gave it five minutes; and if Grace wanted to kick my ass, she'd have to catch me first.

I found her place easily enough, a nice little bungalow in Atascadero with a detached garage and some kind of studio or guest quarters above that. There was no sign of her car but it was probably in the garage. The good news was I didn't see the town car either.

The door was answered by an attractive woman who

looked to be about Sydney's age. Wearing some kind of sexy little robe, her hair was tousled and her cheeks were flushed. I didn't know much about lesbian relationships but I knew when a woman was satisfied. How she got that way was something I didn't want to think about. Well, I did but that wasn't the time.

In the blink of an eye, her smile turned into a scowl that made my balls draw up. And not in a good way. "What do you want, Mr. Dunham? Didn't you shoot your mouth off enough yesterday or have you replenished your vitriol and want another go at her?"

This was one pissed-off female, but for the moment my confusion trumped my fear. "Have we met?"

"No, thank God, but Sydney's described you right down to your stupid eyebrows." She squinted and got up on her tiptoes for a closer look. "Do you tweeze or wax?"

Criticizing my communication skills was one thing but taking potshots at my manhood was cold. "Look, Annette…"

"Amanda."

"Amanda, sorry. Is Sydney here?"

"No, she left here over an hour ago with some empty boxes. I assumed she was going to the office to get her things. How could you do that to her? Yesterday morning she was as happy as I've ever seen her. And then last night she was…"

"I agree in hindsight we could have handled the situation better but those aren't guidelines in the contracts, they're rules, rules that are there for a reason. Using herself as bait, regardless of the outcome, was…"

"Was what, Mr. Hot Shot Investigator? I don't see you or your organization out there in the trenches, putting your asses on the line to save lives, not unless it comes with a hefty paycheck."

We glared at each other for a couple of seconds before she grabbed my hand and pulled me inside the house. "There's something you need to see."

Leading me down a hallway, she stopped outside a room and opened the door. The space was tiny, not much larger than a walk-in closet. With little more than a desk and a computer inside, it was cramped and stuffy. But it was the walls that stunned me. Hundreds, perhaps thousands of eyes stared back at me from headshots, mostly women and children.

"Who are they?"

Amanda sighed and leaned into the doorframe. "They're the ones who don't make the evening news or twenty-four/ seven cable shows, the ones who don't have families with the time and money to keep their stories out there. Many come from poor families or foster care, strippers, prostitutes, runaways. But the one thing they have in common is that they're missing and no one's looking for them. When she isn't working for you, this is Sydney's life. She's online every night, sometimes till one or two in the morning, with the North American Missing Persons Network or the Doe Network, trying to match photographs with composites done from remains. She also tries to stay on top of current cases but there are too many of them. The case in San Francisco was one of the exceptions. She profiled that bastard after the second woman went missing. As it turns out, she was right."

In my line of work, I wasn't easily surprised. But this? "Why does she do this?"

"It's personal with her. We were in college when a writer she respected was brutally murdered. It was in the summer of 2001, July I think, and then 911 happened and everyone's attention was elsewhere. Sydney was headed for law school but she changed her major to forensic science after the murder."

I got a whiff of Sydney's scent, soap and vanilla. My knees buckled and my cock twitched. I had it bad. "She does this every night? When does she sleep?"

Of all the questions I'd thrown at her, this one made her uncomfortable. "She has difficulty sleeping. She has nightmares, bad ones."

I knew enough not to press that particular point but I wanted to know more. "I don't suppose you have any coffee. I know Sydney drinks that damn green tea but…"

"But it smells like donkey piss and tastes even worse. I tell her the same thing."

Maybe we were getting use to one another but Amanda and I were no longer sniping at each other. In fact, if things were different, I might have liked her. The problem was, with every passing minute and every revelation I got in a little deeper. Sydney Forrest was a complicated woman, beautiful, compassionate and sexy as hell. And I could guarantee if I were the one crawling between the sheets with her, she'd be sleeping like a baby every night.

The closer we got to the kitchen, the more Amanda appeared agitated. By the time we settled around the table, she was jumping out of her skin. With everything else going on, I'd almost forgotten about the state of her undress and post-coital glow until a voice, a distinctly male voice, reached us from the other side of the house.

"Woman, bring me food and drink and I shall fuck thy golden orbs."

To her credit, Amanda didn't blink. She colored slightly, raised a hand and flipped it toward the voice, effectively dismissing it. "He's a friend. We're rehearsing a scene from *The Taming of the Shrew*."

"Uh huh. I'm no Shakespearean scholar but I'm fairly certain the Bard never dropped the F-bomb."

That time she blinked.

"What's going on, Amanda?"

She let her breath out in a prolonged sigh. "I guess it doesn't matter now anyway. The genius in the bedroom is my husband. Sydney's not gay."

I tried to concentrate on what she was saying but the *Hallelujah Chorus* in my head was making it difficult to focus.

When I was able to get my own breathing under control, I asked the question. "Why the charade?"

"It was my idea. Sydney had a rough time at Quantico. One of her supervisors was obsessed with her and put her through hell. The Bureau didn't want to hear about it. Instead of dealing with him, they suggested she hire a bodyguard. That was the last straw. Right before she flew out here for her initial interview with you, we were sitting around the dinner table and I jokingly suggested she lay the groundwork that she was gay."

I sensed there was more to the story but I didn't want to rush her. From the way she was avoiding eye contact with me, I also got the feeling I wasn't going to like whatever she was holding back.

When she started talking again, her voice was tentative. "About a week after she started with IIF, she came home and announced she was going to come clean with you and Dr. Hunt, that the men she worked with were very different from the ones at Quantico. She said there was one man in particular whom she was developing feelings for, the first man who ever made her feel safe. I was blown away. Because of her father, she's avoided men and relationships ever since I've known her. After a couple of weeks, I broached the subject again but she said it was no longer an issue, that the man wasn't interested in her so there was no point in rocking the boat and admitting she'd lied."

Dylan. It had to be Dylan. He could be a cold sonofabitch.

"But she was wrong, wasn't she, Mr. Dunham? You do care for her."

My jaw hit the top of table.

"I'll take that as a yes. Then why…Oh, my God. All this time you had feelings for her but you didn't act on them because you thought…"

"Let's just leave it at the fact that I'm an asshole and not replay the last three months, shall we? If she's not here and she's not at the office, where would she go, especially if she were upset?"

"Upset?"

"Her father was just leaving my office as she was arriving this morning. There was an altercation in the parking lot and he hit her."

Amanda jumped to her feet. "And you're just now telling me this? Those should have been the first words out of your mouth."

"Calm down. I'll find her."

"Don't tell me to calm down. You don't know that bastard and what he's done to her. All her life, he's belittled her, made her feel inadequate and stupid. Those nightmares she has? He's hitting her and calling her horrible names."

I'd known my share of rage but the feelings coursing through me were palpable, living things. One way or another, I'd make the bastard pay. "What about her mother?"

"Lady Helena? She's as bad as he is. She has three addictions, alcohol, Botox and shopping. As long as Roger keeps her in two of the three, things are cool around the Forrest manse. Sydney was the only one from our graduating class at Vassar whose parents didn't show up. Because she didn't want to go to law school, he cut off her funds to grad school. She paid for that herself."

I'd heard enough, more than enough. "Amanda, think. You know her better than anyone, where would she go?"

"Probably to Cambria, either the cemetery or Moonstone Beach."

"Why the cemetery?"

"The writer I mentioned, Theresa Ryan, she's buried there. Sydney's gone there before when she's had to think something out. She says it's soothing. We need to split up. I'll have Mike throw on some clothes and go to the cemetery. You go to Moonstone Beach and I'll stay here in case she comes home. Don't fuck this up, Mr. Dunham. Sydney's fragile right now."

"Fragile? I watched her take down a two hundred pound man with a karate kick that I'd have trouble executing. Where the hell did she learn to do that?"

"Um, she has a black belt in Karate. It's not something she likes to broadcast."

Okay, to sum up. I'd fallen for a woman who was a combination of Pippi Longstocking, Wednesday Addams and Jackie Chan. Did I know how to pick 'em or what?

6

Forgive many things in others; nothing in yourself.
— *Ausonius, Latin Poet*

I sensed him before I actually saw him or maybe I heard his car door slam. When I turned around to look, he was negotiating the rocky incline leading to the beach. If I really wanted to, I had plenty of time to scurry up the rocks and be in my car before he made it down. But I didn't. I was there first. He could find his own damn beach.

Reclining on my elbows, my feet freed from the dreadful desert boots, I let my pink-tipped toes wiggle in the sand. On the outside, I was the picture of nonchalance. On the inside, I was vacillating between anger that he'd found me and joy that he'd gone to the trouble.

He settled in next to me and plopped a plastic bag

from a convenience store between us. When it was obvious he wasn't going to explain his appearance, I launched the opening salvo. "How'd you find me?"

"I'm a trained investigator, sweetheart, it's what I do."

"Right." I looked pointedly at the bag. "Someone once said beware of Greeks bearing gifts."

"Everyone credits Virgil with that quote but it was really Jackie Onassis. And anyway, I'm not Greek. I'm Irish, Welsh and English."

He examined the bruise on my arm and grazed the side of my face with the tips of his fingers. I flinched not from the pain inflicted by my father's class ring but because of the electric jolt his touch sent through my body.

He didn't speak, just reached in the bag, pulled out some ice and dropped it into a sandwich bag.

In times of stress I tend to giggle inappropriately, which is exactly what I did. He reminded me of an overgrown Boy Scout, always prepared.

He put the baggie against my face and brought my hand up to hold it in place. "You won't find it so funny when you wake up in the morning and your face is puffy and turning all kinds of disgusting colors. Now hold that there and don't take it off until I tell you to."

This time I beat him to the punch and arched an eyebrow of my own. "Here's the thing. I no longer work for you which means I don't have to take orders from you. It's one of the perks of my termination."

He was looking at me with the same expression I'd seen the day before in Dylan's office, the one that made me squirm. I couldn't help it. I caught myself looking right back at him and thinking he was the most handsome man I'd ever seen.

"Sydney, we have to talk."

They were the perfect words at the perfect moment. Had he said anything else, I might have crawled in his lap and cried like a baby. I snapped out of my lovesick stupor and stared at the water. "Is there something to drink in that bag?"

He snapped his fingers. "Thanks for reminding me. I'm sure you'd prefer hot donkey piss but cold was the best I could do."

Donkey piss. Clever man. He was letting me know he'd spoken to Amanda and the jig was officially up. "So Amanda spilled her guts. What did you do, water-board her?"

"Technically, she spilled *your* guts. And before you open that beautiful mouth again and say something that's going to thoroughly piss me off, understand that I'm hanging here by a thread and you're one smart-ass comment away from me pulling you across my knee and tanning your hide."

My tummy quivered and my panties flooded but I kept my mouth shut.

"You lied to us and because of that lie I wasted three months of my life wanting something I thought I couldn't have. Under the best of conditions, I'm a sonofabitch, demanding and possessive, but because of that lie I became someone even I didn't recognize. That's the reason I yanked Jared out of Bahrain and replaced him. I figured if I couldn't stand myself, no one else could either. And then yesterday I came back and the first thing I saw was a woman, my woman, buck-ass naked on a stage putting her life in danger. Except she's not my woman because I'm still believing the lie. But today? Today I found out she had feelings for me all along, that instead of dodging camel shit, we could have been loving one another into oblivion and fucking like bunny rabbits."

My woman. I listened to him, my heart hammering in my ears. Everything I wanted was within my reach, so naturally I pushed it away. One thing I'd discovered about the universe was its insistence on symmetry, yin and yang, life and death, sadism and masochism. My father was a sadist and I, his child, the masochist.

"I'll admit I had a crush on you but that's all it was. I got over it when you left the country. Besides, my father wouldn't permit it. He'd break you."

He found that funny. "Break me?"

"It's what he does, he breaks things. He wouldn't rest until he found a way to punish me by destroying you, Dylan and everything you've worked for."

"Is that what this is about? Honey, believe me when I say we serve at the pleasure of people way above his pay grade. Your daddy snarled at the wrong dogs."

I had no idea what he meant by that. All I knew was that I had to end things and quickly. If my only option was to reveal the secret parts of myself, then so be it. "You don't want me, Jordan, I'm damaged. He broke me too."

He studied my face for a long few moments before he ran his hand up my neck and through my hair. Cradling my head in his hand, he skimmed his lips over mine. "We're all damaged, sweetheart. The trick is finding the one person in the world who can put us back together."

"There isn't enough glue on the planet to put me back together. An hour ago, I was sitting in a cemetery talking to a woman who's been dead for ten years."

"A lot of people talk to the dead. We'll worry about it when she starts talking back."

I pushed him away with a force that shocked us both. "There is no *we*. *We* don't exist. I don't love you, Jordan. I thought I did at one time but I don't anymore." Jumping to my feet, I landed the final blow. "You were right about the disc. I sent it. I have a job offer in Europe and I'm taking it. I leave tomorrow."

The hurt on his face morphed to puzzlement as he narrowed his eyes and stared at something in the distance, the copse of trees near the shoreline. With his attention elsewhere, I seized the moment and ran. Reaching the top of the rocks, I looked frantically for my car. Why had I parked so far away? I started to run again but slowed when I heard the sound. It was faint but distinctive, in a place where it didn't belong. Wind chimes. Now I knew for certain I was going mad.

Still twenty feet from my car, the sound stopped me in my tracks and I turned to look down the rocks at Jordan. I needed him, needed him to hold me and tell me I wasn't crazy. If he were coming for me, I'd wait for him. But he wasn't moving. He wasn't even looking at me. He didn't want me after all.

Those were my last thoughts before I was thrown forward and the ground rose up to meet me. Before everything went black.

7

I was in some fucked up slow-motion nightmare. Just seconds before the explosion, I saw her running to her car, copper hair flying, catching the glint of the sun, but something grabbed my attention and I looked away.

I remember climbing the rocks, dodging burning red chunks of her Fiat. I was praying, yelling her name and thinking I'd lost her. The bile rose in my throat as I took in the devastation. And then I saw her on the ground and relief and confusion muddled my ability to think. At the speed she was running, she should have been in the car. Why wasn't she?

All this was going through my head as I dropped to my knees beside her. Blood was leaking through her tank top and

I pulled it up as gently as I could. Her back had taken the worst of it, a few small shards of glass and bits of metal. I took the time to run my fingers against her scalp and felt nothing but soft strands of silk.

She was like a doll in my arms as I carried her to my SUV and laid her on her stomach in the backseat. Making sure her head was turned so she could breathe, I covered her, jumped in the front and gave it the gas. I broke every law in the book, including leaving the scene of a crime, but I couldn't care less. I was flying blind but I knew three things: automobiles don't spontaneously combust, someone was trying to kill the woman I loved and I would move heaven and earth to keep her safe.

My training kicked in and I organized my thoughts. In less than a minute, I had Dylan on a disposable cell phone I kept just in case. "Get the jet in the air and meet me at SLO airport in forty minutes. Bring your medical bag. I'm just leaving Cambria. I've got Sydney in the backseat and she's out cold with lacerations on her back from flying debris, mostly metal and glass. I can't tell if there are any internal injuries but I doubt it."

His voice came through loud and clear. "Hold on."

I waited while he put the wheels in motion. When he came back on the line, he sounded tense. "Is there a reason you're not taking her to a hospital?"

"Yeah, there is. Her Fiat's scattered all over Moonstone Beach and it wasn't an accident. If whoever did this suspects she's not dead, hospitals are the first place they'll look."

"What's the plan?"

"I'm taking her to Tahoe. Call my sister and ask her to pick up food and supplies for at least a week and drop them at the cabin. Make sure she gets tea bags, green tea. And say please."

"A week?"

"As long as it takes to figure out who did this and why."

"And what is the lovely Dr. Forrest going to say when she discovers she's alone with you in the middle of nowhere?"

"I can only imagine." Something clicked in my brain and I grabbed it before I lost it. "Have Scotty go outside and gather up the cigarette butts around where that asshole was standing today, Forrest's goon."

"You can't seriously believe Forrest would try to murder his own daughter?"

"I know what I saw and someone was watching us from the trees near the waterline. Could be he used a remote to detonate the device. The cops will be all over the place tonight but in the morning have some guys search the area for anything suspicious. It's about five hundred yards to the right of where the car exploded."

"Anything else?"

"Yeah. Sydney had an obsessed fan at Quantico, one of her supervisors. According to her roommate, the guy didn't even get a slap on the wrist but I'd like to know where he was this afternoon."

"Her roommate?"

It slipped my mind that we hadn't spoken since that morning, so he was in the dark about recent developments. "Yes, her roommate, her married roommate. Sydney's straight." *And she's mine.*

The bastard had the nerve to chuckle. "So that's how it is."

"That's how it is. You have a problem with that?"

"No problem here, amigo. I just wish I'd known first."

8

A woman can forgive a man for the harm he does her... but she can never forgive him for the sacrifices he makes on her account.
—W. Somerset Maugham, The Moon and Sixpence

What little I recalled came in snippets, running, falling, Jordan yelling my name. After that, nothing.

I lay there for awhile, until I could open my eyes without feeling nauseous. It was only a sliver of light that split the darkness, a door to an adjoining room left ajar, but it was enough to make me queasy. Whispered voices reached my ears, familiar voices, but the words were impossible to discern above the ringing in my ears and the pounding of my head.

My brain told me to get up, confront the voices and demand answers but my body rebelled. It was happy right where it was. Tears stung my cheeks and I found comfort in the pillow, the cotton cool against my skin.

When I awoke again, it was daylight and my eyes adjusted slowly. The voices I'd heard the night before were clearer but distant, no longer just beyond the door.

Throwing back the covers, I managed to sit up. Standing was more difficult but once I steadied myself, I found I could walk without wobbling. I made a beeline for what I hoped was a bathroom and locked the door behind me. I had to pee and didn't want someone wandering in. I avoided the mirror as long as I could. When I finally summoned the courage, it was worse than I imagined. I was what the cat dragged in, mauled and dragged back out.

As I washed my hands, I stared at the basket on the counter, an enormous basket filled with fresh supplies of everything a guest would need to feel at home, especially female guests, all the usual things including tampons. Rifling through the items, I plucked a bottle of shampoo from its nest, my brand and even my fragrance, vanilla. With all the brands available, I found that curious but no more surprising than standing nude in a strange bathroom. And yes, I was nude. Someone had undressed me, a fact that bothered me far less than it should have.

I was prolonging the inevitable but I needed and wanted a shower. Groggy, teary and wretched was not the image I wanted to project when I faced my captors, the same men who had fired me, watched my humiliation at the hands of my father, threatened me with a spanking and carted me off to God-knew-where.

I was sick of playing defense, of playing the victim, sick of the nightmares and the memories lying just beyond my reach. I was sick of wanting something I couldn't have and the fear that kept me prisoner. I was sick of me.

My back burned with the sting of a thousand bees as I stepped from the shower and used whatever items I could find to fix the damage. I brushed, swished, flossed and powdered. Clothes were problematic. I had nothing. After pawing through the drawers in the bedroom, I found just enough to preserve what little dignity I had left, a pair of plaid boxer shorts and a wife-beater top, both miles too big. The clothes held on with safety pins and my hair pulled up in a scrunchie, I risked a final glance in the mirror and groaned. It was just the look I was going for, Pebbles Flintstone on crack.

Emerging from the bedroom, I took the time to admire the space. The view from floor-to-ceiling windows was breathtaking. High in the trees and about as isolated as one could be, the A-frame structure looked out over a lake, one I didn't recognize.

The smell of cooking coaxed a rumble from my stomach and I followed my nose. As I suspected, Dylan and Jordan were seated at the table. Looking cool, confident and cocky, their mouths dropped open when they saw me, which was all I needed to set me off.

"Where the fuck am I?!" Stomping my foot was overkill but when you're five-foot-four and intent on going head to head with men well over six feet, I knew I had to grab their attention from the get-go.

Always the professional, Dylan was the first to recover. He pulled out a chair, eased me into it and started to check my pulse.

I slapped his hand away. "Stop that, I'm fine."

Jordan was smiling at me, an evil little smile that made me feel flushed. "You look fine to me, sweetheart, but let him check you over. Are you hungry?"

Yes, I'm starving. "No, thank you. I just want to know where I am and why I'm here."

"You're at Lake Tahoe. We flew you here yesterday after the problem with your car. You've been asleep almost eighteen hours."

That wasn't possible. Eighteen hours was more sleep than I usually got in a week. "I don't understand. If there was a problem with my car, why didn't you just call AAA or have it towed somewhere?"

Taking the seat next to me, Dylan grabbed my hands and held them loosely in his. "What do you remember about yesterday, honey, about going to Moonstone Beach?"

I didn't want to think about that let alone talk about it.

Jordan sensed my hesitancy and jumped in with both feet. "He knows about us, Sydney. Tell him what you remember."

I wanted to scream at him *there is no us* but this wasn't the time or the place. "I like it there. I went to say good-bye." I searched my tone for signs of self-pity but found none. It was a statement of fact.

"Good-bye?" Dylan sounded surprised.

"Yes, good-bye." I looked directly at Jordan. "I told you yesterday, I have a job offer in Europe and I'm taking it."

He leaned forward and rested his elbows on his thighs. "We know your father sent the disc. When this whole mess is over, we want you back."

Pieces of the puzzle fell in place, his going to the house and talking to Mandy, showing up at the beach, all of it. "Why, to spite my father? He wants me gone so you want me back? I'm a human being, not a chess piece in some alpha male pissing contest."

"You just mixed a metaphor, sweetheart, and you can't possibly believe what you just said."

"You have no idea what I'm capable of believing, either of you."

His expression turned dark. "Then believe this. Someone rigged your car to explode with you in it. The fact that you weren't in it was a miracle, that and the fact that you sustained only a couple of minor cuts to your back. We also think whoever did it was watching you from the trees at Moonstone Beach with a remote control in his hand. I saw you running, Sydney. You should be dead right now. What made you stop and turn around? When I found you, you were facing away from the car."

"I don't remember." It was a lie, but in my defense I was on information-overload. I knew what I heard but no one would believe me. At the moment, understanding why I wasn't dead was more important than learning someone had gone to a lot of trouble to ensure I wound up that way.

Dylan was standing behind me. "Lean forward so I can raise your top and check your back. I had to remove some bits and pieces of glass and metal. I'm leaving a prescription for pain killers. J.D. said you have trouble sleeping. Do you want me to write a prescription for a mild sleeping pill?"

I shook my head, unable to form the words. All of a sudden, I felt cold and very, very alone.

Jordan was on his knee in front of me, using the pads of his thumbs to wipe away my tears, tears I had no idea I was spilling. "It's going to be all right, baby. We'll figure this out and keep you safe from everyone, including your father. No one will ever hurt you again."

No one but you. When you find out I'm not the person you think I am, when I can't love you the way you want and need to be loved, you'll hurt me, Jordan. And that hurt will never heal.

Dylan slapped his thighs and rose from his chair. "Well, you two kids play nice and Uncle Dylan will go back and catch the bad guys."

I got to my feet. "Give me five minutes and I'll be ready to go with you."

"Sweetheart, the chances of your going anywhere, particularly with me, are slim to no fucking way."

"But…" I looked from one man to the other and the bastards were grinning. And on top of everything else, my ass was starting to throb.

Watching me rub it, Dylan favored me with one of his thousand-watt smiles. "I've given you several shots, including tetanus and a couple for pain, and I'm here to tell you that seeing it on film cannot compare to seeing it in the flesh. You truly have one of the finest butts it's ever been my privilege to inject."

I could have sworn I heard Jordan growl which was just too weird. Sometimes late at night when I couldn't sleep, I indulged my fondness for paranormal erotica and downloaded an e-book. At least once a page, the hero/shifter would emit a growl, usually when his woman was threatened. I'd play their game and be their damsel in distress, for a few days anyway. But if Jordan started howling at the moon, I was going to seriously lose it.

9

I was an animal. From the second she stepped into the kitchen looking pouty and adorable, I wanted to throw her down on the table and bury my cock in her so deep we'd need the Jaws of Life to remove it. I didn't care that some bastard was trying to kill her, didn't care that she was bruised and battered. By the time I was finished with her, she wouldn't care either.

But my baser instincts would have to wait. Amanda was right. Sydney was fragile. Buried beneath the kick-ass scientist and Ninja warrior, the compassionate and loyal friend, there was a wounded woman with secrets, ones I needed to plumb before I could truly make her mine.

It wouldn't be easy. Thanks to her father and God only

knew how many other men, she'd built up a maze of defenses to keep herself safe. I sensed them at the beach. I saw the way she looked at me and turned away, felt her lean into my fingers as I grazed her cheek, heard the barely-there whimper when I pulled back. I even smelled the delicate scent of her arousal when I threatened to spank her, the benefits of which I had every intention of introducing her to down the line.

When she admitted her feelings for me, the words leached into my soul like water to a thirsty man, but just as quickly the curtain came down and she ran. Here there would be no running away. I had all the time in the world to learn her secrets, take them as my own and earn her trust.

I walked Dylan to the rental car, chatted a few more minutes and tromped around outside double-checking security. I was giving her time to digest what was happening, but I needed time as well. I had to get into character, to turn from caring lover to bad-ass bodyguard from hell. She wasn't going to be happy with me but that couldn't be helped. Things needed to be said and rules laid down. As much as I cared about her and wanted her happy, above all I wanted her safe. When I took that sweet ass, I wanted it in one piece.

Unfortunately, the best way to do that was keep her off-balance and scared shitless. It was a lousy thing to do but I had no choice. This wasn't my first experience with guarding a near-miss victim and I knew my job well. If I let my feelings for her override my instincts and training, we could both wind up dead. If we stayed alive, I'd have a lifetime to make it up to her.

If I were honest, there was another reason I wanted to morph into super-prick and there was nothing even remotely noble in my motives. I wanted to push her limits and test her mettle. I wanted to help turn her sadness into rage and her prudence into passion. I wanted to know what made her tick and what ticked her off. I'd seen glimpses of anger but that's all they were, tiny sparks. I wanted the whole package. I wanted the fireworks.

When I walked back in the kitchen, she was still at the table but she'd poured herself a large mug of coffee. She held it in both hands and looked about twelve with her face scrubbed clean and my clothes swamping her body. Her enormous blue eyes looked up at me over the rim of the mug, uncertain and frightened, and I almost came in my jeans. In all my life, I'd never seen anything more perfect.

"There are tea bags in the pantry if you'd prefer that, green tea."

"Thanks but I think I need the caffeine. It isn't every day you find out someone wants you dead."

"I'm not going to let anything happen to you, Sydney. I've told you that. Did you find everything you needed in the bathroom? If not, make a list and I'll pick it up when I go into town for your prescription."

"You thought of everything. I'm sure your other female

guests are equally impressed."

I detected a hint of jealousy and my dick bobbed its approval while I attempted to keep a shit-eating grin off my face. "As much as I'd like to take the credit, I called ahead and had one of my sisters make a drugstore run. She's also the one who picked up the tea."

She wet her lips. "Your sister lives here?"

"About twenty minutes away. My grandfather started buying up land around Lake Tahoe in the fifties. My parents, my other sister and her family and my baby sister all have homes around the lake. When my dad owned the vineyard, they were used as summer homes, a place to escape to when the heat in Paso got too bad. When he sold the vineyard a few years back, they winterized them and everyone moved here year-round. Dylan and I worked on this one on and off over the years."

"You built this? It's beautiful, what I've seen of it."

"We don't get a chance to use it much. More often than not, it's used as a safe house. We had a family of four living here for a month last year."

"Thank your sister for me."

"You can thank her yourself. I talked to my folks a little while ago and they invited us for dinner tomorrow night. I'm sure they think you'll want a break after being cooped up with me for two days. It's just my family, but you'll need something to wear other than that. We're a pretty casual group but I don't want to share you in that outfit, so you'll have to trust me to pick something out when I'm in town."

She paled visibly. "Family?"

"Family, sweetheart, the people who pissed you off when you were growing up but who loved you unconditionally and still take an interest in what's going on in your life."

"I'll have to take your word for that."

I could have kicked myself. If they gave awards for insensitivity, I was a shoe-in.

"Jordan, I can't stay here and jeopardize you and your family. Amanda can wire me money and send my passport. I'll leave the country. I can hide and no one will find me. Oh, my God, Amanda. She's probably worried sick. I have to call her."

Mr. Nice Guy left the building. "I realize you've been through a rough few hours but you're going to sit there and listen to me and not speak until I'm finished. You're not going anywhere except back to bed or the sofa. Your body's still recovering from the effects of the blast and whether or not you think you've had enough rest, I don't, and my opinion is the only one that matters from here on out. As far as putting me and my family in jeopardy, that's not your problem. When Dylan and I started IIF ten years ago, my family made the decision to cover the tracks of the land purchases made by my grandfather and add extra security. Even your father wouldn't be able to follow the paper trail. As to calling or emailing anyone, not happening. Dylan's already spoken to Amanda and Mike and they're upset but they also know you're in good hands. Thomas has moved into the guest quarters over your garage and will be there twenty-four seven until we catch the bastard."

"You think whoever did it might try to get to me through them?"

"This is what we do, Sydney, and we do it very well. And the reason we're able to do it very well is because our clients have the good sense to follow the rules. Since I know from recent experience that following the rules isn't your strong suit, I'm going to be watching you like a hawk."

Her cheeks blossomed red, her pupils dilated and she jumped from her chair. I was about to be ripped a new asshole.

"Really. You do realize that technically I'm not your client and I could get up and walk out of here and there's nothing you could do about it. Furthermore, if you're referring to my recent appearance at *Naughty Nellie's*, I hope you kept a copy for yourself because that's the only way you'll ever see me naked again."

God, I loved that woman. "And technically I could have you stripped in about five seconds, tie you to my bed and ravage your little body for the next few weeks and not only would no one know, no one would hear you scream."

"If you think you can bully me by…"

Sometimes actions speak louder than words and that was one of those times. Before she knew what was happening, I lifted her to the countertop, spread her legs so I could move in closer and had both her hands held behind her back with one of mine. I cupped her face with my other hand and swept my lips lightly back and forth across hers until she opened for me. And when she did, it was the sweetest mouth I'd ever tasted. My tongue explored every detail, the ridges and hollows, the evenness of her small white teeth, the softness of her tongue as it danced with mine. When she whimpered and ground her pussy against my cock, I pulled back, steadied her and kissed her on the nose. "Go take a nap. I'll wake you up when lunch is ready and this time you're going to eat or I'll force-feed you. And you're coming with me when I go into town. I don't trust you any farther than I can throw you. Now scoot."

She jumped down from the countertop and wiped her mouth with the back of her hand. "Don't do that again, Jordan. This thing you think we have, whatever it is, is never going to happen."

This time she didn't run. She walked away from me and I knew she believed what she said. There was something in the set of her shoulders and the defiant lift of her chin that chilled me to the bone. And for the first time, I started to think she was right.

10

Forgiveness is almost a selfish act because of its
immense benefits to the one who forgives.
—*Lawana Blackwell, The Dowry of Miss Lydia Clark*

I have no idea how long I sat perched on the edge of the bed. Minutes, hours? I tried to keep my mind blank, to concentrate on other things, anything to steer my thoughts from the kitchen, from the way he took control, the feel of his mouth and the way I responded and rubbed myself against him, wanting him inside me.

It should have been easy. Over the months, I'd developed techniques for keeping thoughts of him at bay. This time I tried reciting the Pledge of Allegiance backwards. When that didn't work, I lay back and slid my hand inside the waistband of the shorts. I was still sopping wet. I closed my eyes and pictured his face as my fingers found my clit. Within seconds, it was over, a small release but better than nothing. Not that I had a frame of reference.

A door slammed somewhere in the house and I sat up. Was he leaving for town and decided not to take me? Who could blame him? Or perhaps he hoped I'd seize the opportunity and slip away. He could convince himself that he'd done the right thing in bringing me here, keeping me out of harm's way, but everyone knew I had a mind of my own and didn't follow rules. *Hell, I don't know, Dylan. I just stepped out for a few minutes and when I got back she was gone. You know Sydney. She's more trouble than she's worth. I gave it my best shot, amigo, but we have to let her go. She'll be fine.*

But I wouldn't be fine, not without him, not anymore. He cared about me too, I knew he did. At least he did before I wiped his kiss away and spoke my ridiculous exit line. At that point, it was ludicrous to deny what was happening. I loved him madly. Now the only question that remained was if he believed what he said to me on the beach. *The trick is finding the one person in the world who can put us back together.* Yes, I was damaged and inexperienced and rather a mess but I wanted to be whole, to be the woman I saw reflected in his eyes.

Too much thinking made me drowsy and I yawned. *Bitch. Cunt. Whore.* This time the words didn't faze me. My father was my past. The Prince of Darkness was my future.

I must have slept like the dead. When I woke up, I was

covered with a quilt and at the foot of the bed was a stack of new clothes, all neatly folded, two pair of jeans, some tank tops and shorts and a shirred skirt that would hang to mid-calf, the exact color of my eyes. He'd thought of almost everything, including a pair of pajamas in soft, soft flannel. The only thing missing was underwear which I suspected was more intentional than accidental. My breasts weren't large by any means but they were definitely there and my nipples were hyper-sensitive to everything, especially when Jordan was staring at me, something he tended to do a lot.

I freshened up and slipped on a pair of jeans and one of the new tank tops, both of which fit me better than most of my own clothes. Even the pair of sandals he'd bought was my size. Feeling better than I had a right to, considering where I was and why, I left my prison cell to claim my fate.

He was standing at the stove, his back to me, and I took a moment to admire the view. If there were a more beautiful male specimen on earth, I didn't want to know about it. Jordan was delicious, every sinful inch of him. He was all magnificent male, and if I hadn't already blown it, he was mine. "May I help?"

"I was beginning to think I was going to have to perform CPR on you."

I tried not to let his frosty tone discourage me. He had every right to be angry. "Thank you for the clothes, I love them. How did you know my size?"

"You're not the first woman I've bought clothes for, Sydney."

Wow, low blow. "I'm sure that's true." I was new to this whole relationship thing so I wasn't sure the acceptable amount of time to let him vent his spleen before I picked up the nearest breakable object and aimed it at his head.

"But you're the first woman I've ever wanted to buy clothes for, although if I had my way I'd keep you naked for the next fifty years or so."

I was so relieved, my whole body went limp. "Really?"

He took a seat at the table and pulled me into his lap. "Yes, really, you little brat. And if you ever wipe off one of my kisses again, I'll…"

"Tan my hide?"

"I plan to do that anyway whenever the spirit moves me or you get out of line. What I was going to say is the next time you wipe off one of my kisses, you won't get another one for at least an hour."

Encircling his neck, I nuzzled into him. I'd never smelled anything so good in my life. "By definition, I think that's considered cruel and unusual punishment."

"Sue me." He sniffed the air and kissed me quickly on the lips. "Dinner's burning."

Reluctantly, I slipped off his lap and started setting the table. "What happened to lunch?"

"You slept through it, sweetheart, another eight hours. On

top of the eighteen you slept yesterday, you've now officially slept around the clock." He dug into the pocket of his jeans and pulled something out. "I forgot to give you these this morning. I took them off you yesterday when we undressed you."

My watch and my locket. I sometimes forgot to put on my watch but I was never without the locket. I must have been out of it if I hadn't noticed it was gone. "Thank you."

"Pretty locket. Do you have a thing for hummingbirds?"

No, I just wear one around my neck to remind me of the most horrible period of my life. I gave you fair warning I'm a nutcase, so back off, Jack.

"I like them, they're sweet. What's for dinner?"

"Lemon chicken, baked potato and Caesar salad. And a humorous little Pinot Grigio I picked up in town."

"Everything sounds yummy except the wine. Alcohol and I don't get along. I hope you don't mind."

"Of course, I don't mind. I'll just have to come up with other ways to seduce you." He must have seen the look on my face because he sat down and tugged me onto his knee again. "That was a joke and not a very good one. You take all the time you need. I'm a very patient guy and you're well worth the wait. I grabbed some movies in town so after dinner we'll settle on the sofa and watch something, your choice."

I pretended to think about it but I'd snuck a peek at the

stack on my way through the great room. "Gosh, I don't know. How about a Clint Eastwood bang-bang-shoot 'em-up."

He curled a finger under my chin and lifted it. "I am so hot for you right now."

11

Anyone who has ever gone to war and witnessed man's inhumanity to man has questioned the existence of God. But there have been three times in my life when I knew with absolute certainty that He existed and was hearing me. The first was when my mother's biopsy came back benign, the second was when I realized Sydney wasn't in her car when it exploded, and the third was when that sweet thing walked into the kitchen, came willingly into my lap and melted in my arms.

I'm a guy, a pretty macho guy at that, so I couldn't let on that I'd just spent the last eight hours fighting the impulse to blow my brains out. It taught me a valuable lesson. Sydney

Forrest would be the death of me, but it would be one hell of a ride.

Over dinner, we made small talk, the kind of chatter couples do on a first or second date. I can't speak for her, but I was already past that, imagining all the things that went with a lifetime commitment, marriage, a home and a couple of kids I was going to enjoy the hell out of planting in her belly.

I'd heard her laughter a couple of times at IIF but nothing compared to hearing it up close and personal. It was a beautiful thing, not prissy and girlie, but full-throated and lusty.

There were a few tense minutes when we talked about the creep in San Francisco and I confessed to knowing her part in his capture. She blushed and blew it off as nothing. That's when I lowered the boom and told her in no uncertain terms her gumshoe stripper days were over, that the only person she'd be performing for was me and I had ways of dealing with disobedience.

Her eyes flew open and for a fraction of a second I wished I'd worn a cup. Then she smiled, bit her puffy lower lip and said, "Yes, sir." And for the second time that day, I almost blew my wad. I was so fucked.

She insisted on cleaning the kitchen and I watched appreciatively as she found her way around. I loved watching her, the way she moved, the way her butt looked in the jeans, the way her breasts bounced in the tank top, her nipples hard as pebbles. Fifteen minutes of that exquisite torture and I was ready for Clint, my second cold shower of the day and the unappealing prospect of sleeping alone.

I have to confess she lasted longer than I would have watching a chick-flick. About an hour into the movie, she kissed me on the cheek and retired to take a bubble bath before bed.

Maybe it was wishful thinking but I could have sworn her ass had a bit more attitude as she walked away from me. Then again, I was randy as a teenager and by that time Clint was looking good.

Had I been looking at her face and not her butt, I might have seen the turmoil lurking just below the surface, the desire warring with her fear. I might have held her a little tighter and told her I loved her and not to be afraid. But I didn't. Macho guy, remember?

It was a mistake I hoped to never make again.

12

Pray you now, forget and forgive.
— *William Shakespeare, King Lear*

It's been said there are defining moments in a person's life that dictate who we are and what we're made of. I wasn't sure about that but I knew without question that I was about to take the most important step of my life and put my trust in someone who had the power to save me or destroy me.

The irony is he had no choice but to follow me down the path, a path so dark I went there only in my nightmares. The decision whether to lead me out or leave me there would be his and his alone.

The hour or so that I waited for the film to end was the longest of my life. After my bath, I listened at the door like a child on Christmas Eve. I heard him remove the DVD, turn off the lights and walk the house ensuring that doors were locked and windows were closed. I heard him walk down the hallway and start the shower in his bathroom. He was in there quite a while and I knew the reason why. The image of him, the water running in rivulets down his body, his muscles straining as he brought himself relief was burned into my brain. Was he seeing my face as I had seen his only hours before? God, I hoped so.

When I no longer heard the water, I returned to my perch on the edge of the bed and waited an additional few minutes. What I had to say could only be said in darkness. Every ounce of my courage would be used to make the walk to his room and tell my story. If I saw pity on his face or anything other than love, I would be more lost than I already was.

The pajamas he'd bought for me were soft against my skin but not the sexiest ones I'd ever seen. It made me love him all the more. He'd been thinking of me, not himself when he bought them, a sleeveless button-up top and boy short bottoms.

If things went the way I prayed they would, I would be out of them within the hour.

His lights were out but his door was open when I rapped on it lightly. "Jordan, may I talk to you?"

"What's wrong, baby, can't you sleep?"

He turned on his bedside light and I saw that he was naked to the waist. Seeing his torso in clothes, even the tight shirts he favored, had not prepared me for the muscular power of his body. If he wanted to, he could break me like a twig, and if I thought too hard about what was concealed beneath the sheet, what I'd felt in the kitchen when I ground against him, I might run out the door and never look back.

"Honey, what is it? Are you all right?"

"Would you mind turning off the light?"

He complied without a moment's hesitation.

I took a breath and wrapped my arms around myself, a childish gesture I'd employed ever since I could remember. And then I started talking.

"I was raped when I was six, someone my father knew. It lasted until I was twelve and started my period. I never saw his face and he rarely spoke. When he did, I didn't recognize his voice. I went to my father and begged him to stop the man but he said I was horrible and bad and it was my fault. He said the man was a friend and wouldn't hurt me unless I told someone. He said no one would believe me anyway, but if they did the police would take me away and put me in an orphanage and no one would want me and I'd die there.

"I never told anyone, but in prep school we were given an assignment to write a short story about a fictitious character who had overcome a traumatic experience and I wrote about a little girl who'd been raped. My teacher didn't believe a fifteen year old could write that authoritatively about something unless she'd been through it. I denied it of course but she reported it anyway. Connecticut Child Protective Services went to our home in Greenwich and questioned my parents. The next day I was pulled out of Choate and that's when the physical abuse began. He said I embarrassed him and jeopardized his career, that the only thing I was good for was a convenient hole for a man's dick."

Jordan cleared his throat. "Are you finished?"

"You haven't heard the best part. I'm not even good for that. I haven't been with a man since I was twelve. I don't know the first thing about pleasing you and I'm scared to death I'll fall apart or do something stupid and you won't want me."

The light went on and I was momentarily blinded. I closed my eyes and rubbed them and when I opened them he was standing in front of me. "There is nothing on God's green earth that could keep me from wanting you. But you have to tell me what you want me to do, sweetheart, because if you don't give me something to do, I'm going to tuck you into bed, get on a plane, hunt down your bastard of a father and kill him with my bare hands. But before I kill him, I'm going to make him tell me the name of the sick fuck who raped you and then I'm going to kill him too. So tell me what you want, right here, right now."

I put my hands on his chest and felt the beating of his heart. "I want you to fix me. I want you to be the first."

I'm still uncertain if that was a slip of the tongue or if I said it to get a reaction. Whichever it was, it earned me a raised eyebrow. "The first and last, baby doll." He started unbuttoning my top. "But we're going to do this my way, nice and slow. If at any time I'm doing something you don't like, tell me and I'll stop. Do you want the light on or off?"

"On, please. I want to see your face. He did it in the dark."

He slid the top off my shoulders and moved his hands slowly down the sides of my breasts. "There is no he. It's just you and me in this room. Keep your eyes open and on mine. All you have to do is go with the sensations and know that I will never hurt you. Can you do that?"

I nodded, unable to speak. His thumbs made lazy circles on my nipples, already engorged from his nearness. As I felt the moisture between my legs, my insides clutched and wanted more. His lips took mine gently, completely, as he lifted me and laid me on the bed. In another instant my shorts were off and he was stretched out beside me.

I took my eyes off his for just a second, long enough to glance down at the monster bumping my thigh. My breath caught. The look on his handsome face was priceless, part lust, part pride. "Relax, we're not there yet."

I wiggled closer to him and his mouth encircled my nipples, alternating between them, licking, sucking, until I thought I would scream. When his hand skimmed my tummy and his fingers nudged my slit, I came up off the bed.

"Christ, you're wet." His fingers eased their way inside me. "You drive the bus, baby, fuck my fingers."

Something snapped inside me and the bogeyman was gone, replaced by the man I loved, the man who knew exactly what I needed and when. I did as he asked, fucked his fingers with a vengeance, fucked them like my life depended on it, all the while his mouth ravaged my nipples and his thumb caressed my clit. And when I came, it was no small release. It was wild and free and beyond anything and everything I'd known. I held his eyes as long as I could and then closed my own. That's when I saw them, thousands of stars lighting my way out of the darkness.

13

My nephew once asked me about the coolest thing I'd ever seen. I put my own spin on *cool* and thought of the things I'd experienced that humbled me and damn near brought me to tears. Hands down, there were two things that stood out. I'd seen the aurora borealis from a dogsled in the Yukon and a sunset in the Serengeti from an open Jeep, but neither of those sights could hold a candle to the woman coming undone before me, trusting me enough to surrender her body and heart in equal measure.

Even my imagination, which tended to work overtime when it came to Sydney, had not been able to conjure the way she arched her back and offered her neck to me, the incredible feel of her skin or the way she murmured my name when she came. The scent that rolled off of her sparked something primal in me, something that begged for scrutiny at another time and place, the need to avenge the pain I'd heard in her voice and the anguish I'd seen on her face.

"Jordan, did I do something wrong?"

I pulled myself back but the damage was done. Her eyes were brimming with tears, tears I'd caused by bringing something ugly into our bed. "Wrong? You're the most right thing I've ever known in my life. I love you, Sydney, and I swear to you I'll make them pay."

She took my face in her hands. "Just love me and fuck me and let them go."

"Yes, ma'am." Her juices were still pouring over my fingers as I pulled them from her and lunged for the nightstand.

When I brought out a condom, she smiled. "Always the Boy Scout."

I went in for another taste of her lips. "We'll have babies, as many as you want, but we'll have them because we planned them. I don't ever want a child of ours thinking it was an accident."

Sheathing myself, I found that even my detour to the dark side hadn't softened my ardor. I was rock hard when I spread her wide and bent her knees. It was then that I added another sight to my list of all-time favorites, her pussy pink, swollen and creaming for me. Being the classy guy I am, the first thing that popped into my head was *breakfast, yum!*

My arms taking the weight of my upper body, my cock was happy as I eased the head through her opening but my brain was sweating bullets. She was small and tight, tighter than anything I was accustomed to. I pushed in a little at a time, pulling out when I thought it was too much. Much to my relief, her concept of slow and easy differed from mine and her channel wanted to swallow me whole. It was when she looked at me shyly, her lashes fluttering, and whispered, "Are we there yet?" and followed it with a giggle that I brought it home.

"Baby, we're going to have to work on that whole giggling thing. There's a time and a place and…"

I don't think she heard me. Her head thrown back, she wrapped her legs around my waist, dug her nails into my shoulders and pitched everything I knew about passion right out the window. Matching me stroke for stroke, that lovely, *fragile* creature turned into a wildcat, giving me the ride of my life and, quite possibly, my death. When I angled just enough to hit her G-spot, we came together in a cacophony of groans, gasps and at least one squeal, probably mine.

Finally able to hold a coherent thought, I disposed of the condom and rolled onto my side, pulling her as close as I possibly could. Her hair brushed my nose and I burrowed into it, inhaling that sweet Sydney smell. "You want to run that whole thing by me again, the part about not being able to please me."

She turned to face me. "I love you, Jordan. I guess that sounds like a cliché after what we just did."

"Well, if it is, you can cliché me any time you have a mind to because I love the sound of it."

She closed her eyes and I did the same, hoping she hadn't retreated from me. I couldn't imagine her pain but I knew it would take time to exorcize it, not just one night in the sack.

Then she smiled and snuggled into me. "I just realized you know almost everything about me, but I know next to nothing about you, except of course that you're dashingly handsome, a brilliant investigator and a fabulous lover. "

"You forgot world-class cook. What else do you want to know?"

She bit her lower lip. I was getting to know her tells and this was one of my favorites. It usually preceded saying something that would get her into deep shit or she was already in it and was buying time to think of a way out. Either way, it was adorable.

"What was she like? Your wife."

Damn, I was good. "Steph was the type that looked great on paper, all-American girl next door, good church-going family, former Girl Scout. We grew up together in Paso Robles, and if you think it's small now, you should have seen it back then. As far as clichés go, we coined the phrase. I was the captain of the football team and she was a cheerleader. Everybody assumed we'd get married. I found out later there were three people who knew it wouldn't work, the three people who knew me the best, my mom, my dad and Dylan. They never trusted her, thought she was devious and manipulative, but they loved me and I thought I loved her so they kept their reservations to themselves. In our second year at Cal Poly, she announced she was pregnant and our folks threw together a quickie wedding. The next day we were driving to San Francisco for a honeymoon when she got her period. Six months after that, she left me a note saying she was going to Palm Springs to visit her aunt for the weekend. By Wednesday when she hadn't called or come home and one of her professors went missing, I put two and two together. I filed for divorce a week later."

"I'm sorry."

"Don't be. It wasn't a marriage made in Heaven, but I have to admit it left me with a few trust issues. Now I live by a simple philosophy. If I can't trust everything a person says, I can't trust anything they say." I felt her body tense and crooked my elbow so I could rest my head on my fist and see her face. Her eyes looked troubled. "Don't ever lie to me, Sydney. That's all I'll ever ask of you. Whatever it is, we'll work through it together but don't ever lie to me."

"Wind chimes."

"What about wind chimes?"

"You asked me this morning why I wasn't in the car when it exploded, why I stopped and turned around. I heard wind chimes, just like I heard them at the cemetery, hundreds of them."

I moved a few strands of hair from her face and swept my thumb over her lower lip. "Wind chimes in a cemetery?"

"The cemetery in Cambria is literally surrounded by trees. Families of those interred there are allowed to hang wind chimes and bird feeders. It's lovely."

"There are some houses across the road from the beach. Maybe you heard wind chimes coming from one of them."

"I thought of that but the sound I heard was different and it wasn't coming from across the road. It was coming from the direction of the water. When I heard them, I stopped running and turned around to look back down at you. I wanted you to come after me."

"I would have if I hadn't been distracted. At that point, I had no intention of ever letting you go, regardless of how much you protested. And, frankly, I don't care why you weren't in that car. If you say you heard wind chimes, that's good enough for me. Tomorrow we'll go out and buy every wind chime we can find and put them on the deck. I'll build an altar to wind chimes. Give me five minutes and I'll write an ode to wind…"

She put a finger to my lips. "I get it. Wind chimes are good."

Since she was the one to bring up Moonstone Beach, I was tempted to ask her a few more questions but Dylan thought we should give her at least another twenty-four hours before bombarding her. Any way I looked at it, the next few days could get ugly. It wasn't every day the daughter of the Deputy Director of the CIA went missing after her car blew up. If it wasn't happening already, *a serious breach in national security* would be streamed on every news channel and screamed by every pundit. There was bound to be a shit storm and I was likely to be in the eye of it. Her poor excuse for a father would like nothing better than to see my ass hung out to dry and my ass was fine right where it was, warm and snug, right smack where it belonged.

Somehow my thumb, the one I'd been swiping against her lower lip, wound up in her mouth and she was sucking on it. I pulled it from between her lips and it came out with a pop. *Holy Mother of God.* And just like that I was hard again, so hard I could have pole-vaulted out of bed.

Against my better judgment, I made a hasty decision. If we were going to survive the maelstrom, we needed to be rested. And if that meant going into the bathroom and slamming my dick between the seat and the toilet bowl, well hell, I'd take one for the team.

Not wanting to appear ungrateful, I rubbed my nose against hers. "Baby, I could go all night but tomorrow the shit's going to hit the fan and we need to be ready for it. Don't move a muscle, I'll be back."

Inside the bathroom, I leaned into the mirror, took several

deep breaths and imagined my folks having sex. Predictably, I went limp as an overcooked noodle. After I urinated, I cleaned myself up and dampened a fresh wash cloth for the little minx in my bed.

She was waiting for me, her face flushed and dreamy, her arms folded behind her head. When she saw the wash cloth, her eyes opened wide but she spread her legs and let me clean her. Midway through the ablutions, I planted another soft kiss on her smooth little pussy. "Damn, honey, we rubbed off all the rhinestones."

That comment earned me one of her lusty laughs and a punch on the shoulder. When I turned her over, she wiggled that glorious ass at me and I thwacked her good, a solid slap to her left butt cheek.

She bolted upright, twisted around and poked me in the chest. "That hurt and you're a brute."

"I meant it to hurt and you're a brat. But I love you with all my heart."

And that earned me a smile that lit up the room.

14

Forgiveness is the answer to the child's dream of a miracle by which
what is broken is made whole again, what is soiled is made clean again.
—Dag Hammarskjöld, Secretary General of the U. N., 1953-1961

The books got it wrong. At that point in the story, the heroine, after two mind-blowing orgasms and a declaration of love from her hero would be sated, exhausted and curled in his arms for the rest of the night. Not me. Oh, I was definitely sated, amazingly and brilliantly so, but I had so much energy I could have painted the house, done a dozen loads of laundry and whipped up enough meals to fill a freezer.

But as I lay there tucked close to his chest, his breath minty and warm against my cheek, I knew when the sun came up I would still be in his arms. And truthfully, there was nowhere else I wanted to be. For the first time in my life, I felt safe and loved. No one would find me, not my father, not the person who wanted me dead, no one.

Too excited to sleep, I replayed every moment since I'd walked into the room, the way my breasts fit his hands when he cupped them, the feel of his thumbs on my nipples, the way he brought me to climax with long, slender fingers that found my secret spots and made them his.

I hadn't wanted it to end. All the wicked things I'd read about, dreamed about, I wanted him to do to me. I wanted him to lay me across his strong, hard thighs and spank me. I wanted to be restrained and forced to do his bidding. I wanted him in my mouth and in my ass. I wanted him to brand me, mark me and claim me as his own. But mostly I wanted him to look at me forever as he'd looked at me tonight, as if I were the center of his universe, as if he'd never let me go.

Forever. That word was lodged deep in my heart and turned my thoughts to Theresa. We'd shared so much, she and I, so much pain and terror but hers didn't end with her childhood. Several years after she published her first book, she too would find the man of her dreams, the man who would make her whole again. But happily ever after wasn't her fate. Mere months into their relationship, he murdered her, just like he'd murdered the others. It would be six long years before they found him, six long years before they discovered her diaries and learned the truth. It was six years too long but I hoped she was finally at peace. For the moment at least, I knew I was.

The room was bathed in morning light when Jordan's hand moved from my waist to my breast, his thumb and forefinger rolling a nipple. I reached down and felt him hard against my thigh. Even with my limited experience, I knew his cock was extraordinary, long and almost as thick as my wrist. A drop of fluid leaked from the head and I touched it with my finger and brought it to my tongue. It tasted sweet and savory and I wanted more.

He moaned and leaned over me, brushing the hair off my face. "Are you sore, baby?"

"No." It was just a little lie, one he wanted to hear.

Breathless, I let him position me. He rolled me over, lifted me to my hands and knees and spread my legs. Sore or not, my body knew what it wanted and I felt the juices running down my thighs. When I heard the drawer open, I sped things along by wiggling my butt at him again, but this time he chuckled and rewarded me by running his hand between my legs.

"Brat."

"Brute."

"You want brute? I can do brute." He slicked his fingers from my pussy and ran them up between the cheeks of my ass. At my anus, he made a small exploration with the tip of his finger and I gasped. "Not so brave now, are you? Don't worry, sweetheart, I have plans for stretching you before I take that sweet hole. Getting there is half the fun."

He rubbed the head of his cock back and forth against my

weeping pussy, always just short of my clit, and I moved my hips trying to make contact. Ever vigilant for bratty behavior, he would have none of that and made his point with another stinging slap.

I didn't dare let on how much I liked that. If I had, he might have stopped what he was doing, and I loved what he was doing. I just wished he were doing it faster. Nevertheless, this time I let him drive the bus, all the while wondering what happened to the nerdy scientist, the woman who avoided men like the plague, the woman who would go to her grave having never been kissed. As his cock entered my channel and I heard his groan of pleasure, I knew exactly what happened to her. She'd died on Moonstone Beach and been reincarnated as a slut, a deliriously happy slut.

As he brought his hands around to my breasts and pinched my nipples, my brain closed down and I was left with a single thought, one that almost made me giggle.

Bring it on, Prince of Darkness. Bring it on!

15

I'm not small in the equipment department and she was damn near a virgin so I knew she was probably sore, but I also knew she wanted me as badly as I wanted her.

This time I intended to take things slowly if it killed me. I had her right where I wanted her. When she started getting frisky, I showed her who was boss. After that, she got with the program and let me do all the work. She took almost every inch of me, and even through the condom I could feel each spasm, each ripple, as she climbed toward release.

I knew I wouldn't last much longer and when she bowed her back and whispered my name, I snaked my hand around to her hard little nub and gave her what she wanted. And God, was it heaven watching her come again as she bucked beneath my hands and milked me dry.

It's not an exaggeration to say I've had my fair share of women. In fact, if I were honest, I've had my share plus ten other guys', but even with her lack of experience, Sydney blew every other woman out of the water.

It wasn't just the exterior stuff either, although that was pretty spectacular. It was the package, her willingness to please, her sense of humor, the way her body responded and prepared itself for me. After almost forty years, I'd finally found the love of my life and she was the best goddamn fuck I'd ever had.

Collapsing in a tangle of arms and legs, I peppered her face with kisses and pulled her back in my arms. "We have a problem, sweetheart. I don't think I'll ever be able to keep my hands off you. The way things are going, we'll have a short but happy life."

The gleam in her eye should have prepared me, but I was still winded from having the top of my head blown off. "Speak for yourself, lover boy. I'm just getting started."

Lover boy? I'd show her lover boy. I figured she had one more climax in her and I wanted breakfast, but before I could throw her onto her back and prove my point, my cell phone rang. The look on her face almost stopped me from answering it. Sadness tinged with fear. Before I even checked the screen, I had to reassure her. "It's okay, baby. Let's just get through this mess and start living that short but happy life." I glanced at the phone. "It's Dylan."

She started to move off the bed but I grabbed her hand. "You don't have to leave."

Squeezing my hand, she tried to form a smile but didn't quite manage it. "I'll take a shower and start breakfast. Thank him for me, for everything."

As the door closed behind her, I hit the talk button. "This better be important."

"How's our girl?" Dylan's day wasn't complete unless he got a rise out of me.

"*My* girl's fine and she was just minutes away from being even finer before you interrupted. What's going on?"

"I got the name of the guy who harassed her at Quantico. There were a number of people who saw it on a daily basis and were willing to go to bat for her but he's well-connected so her complaint went nowhere. Unfortunately, he's not our guy. He was in Virginia when the bombing went down."

"Damn."

"The county's on lockdown as far as any information being released on her car and what caused the explosion, and that includes me, which is unusual to say the least. I'm sure they're keeping a lid on things because of who she is so I'm thinking we're on our own here. I did learn that Forrest chartered a jet out of National and flew directly to San Luis Obispo for his sit-down with you. According to our sources at the airport, about an hour after he left here, the jet took off again for the return trip to D.C. And get this, amigo, he was the only passenger."

"Maybe Smoke Boy came with the car or Forrest hired him from Rent-a-Goon." I was grasping at straws. Chauffeurs didn't usually get involved in family squabbles and there was something in the look on his face when he approached Sydney from behind that said his actions were personal. It was just a gut feeling but my gut was known for being the smartest part about me. If Smoke Boy had flown in with Forrest, why leave him behind? I thought I knew why but even my warped brain couldn't wrap itself around it. *You can't seriously believe Forrest would try to murder his own daughter?* Those were Dylan's words right after the bombing but that was before I knew the truth about Daddy Dearest and how he'd let his baby daughter be raped while he slept down the hall. If we were going anywhere with this, Dylan needed to know everything. The tough part was betraying Sydney's confidence but this was Dylan after all, the guy I trusted with my life and hers.

"You still there, J.D.?"

"Hold on." I got up, went to the door and opened it. When I heard the shower in the other bath, I closed it and started relating the facts as I knew them. "Sydney was raped repeatedly from the age of six until she got her period at twelve. Forrest knew about it, said it was a friend of his. He threatened her if she told anyone. She wrote a short story in high school about

99

a similar incident and the authorities interrogated Forrest and his wife. He started smacking her around after that, so the incident in the parking lot is nothing new. He's been doing it for years."

The silence on the other end spoke volumes and I gave Dylan time to absorb it. When he eventually came back on the line, his voice was low and deadly, as only his tone could get. "That's motive, J.D. If he could allow that to go on under his nose, he's one sick bastard. And if he believed for a moment that she could blow his chances for the Senate, do you really think he'd have any qualms about making her go away permanently? Christ, her death would be just the boon his campaign needed. He'd get the fucking sympathy vote."

Smoke Boy was the key, I was sure of it. "Did our guys find anything at the scene of the explosion?"

"The place is cordoned off tighter than Area 51. We can't get near it. One of the security cameras in our parking lot got a decent shot of him and I emailed it to you about an hour ago. Who knows, maybe Sydney will recognize him. In the meantime, we're trying to get DNA from the cigarette butts he dropped here."

"Keep me posted. How are Amanda and her husband holding up?"

"When I got back here yesterday morning, it occurred to me that when the authorities got around to questioning them, she'd have to tell them she told you where to find Sydney and that would put you at Moonstone Beach when the car exploded. Knowing the way law enforcement works, they'd get fixated on you as a suspect and miss the big picture, especially with you MIA. Before that could happen, I had them flown to Santa Fe along with Thomas to keep an eye on them."

"Thanks for not bringing them here. I've got my hands full as it is."

"I'll bet you do. Listen, J.D., go easy on her. I know you're in pretty deep but she's bound to have baggage, and depending on how much therapy she's had to get past the sexual abuse, it may or may not come back to bite both of you in the ass."

Naturally, my mind went to her extremely bitable ass on the other side of the wall, all soapy and tempting, but I pulled my brain out of the gutter. He had a valid point and I'd learned not to discount his professional opinion. More often than not, he was right. "It's a little late for that. I'm in love with her."

He laughed. "No shit, but I'm glad to hear you admit it. I've waited a lot of years for you to find someone worthy of you. Oh, hey, gotta go. The boys are about to run the *Naughty Nellie's* tape again and I don't want to miss it. I think I smell popcorn."

The line went dead but not before I heard him laugh again. The asshole knew how to yank my chain, I'd give him that.

I was tempted to join her in the shower and make sure she got all the nooks and crannies but the water was already off so I jumped in my own shower. Fifteen minutes later, shaved and dressed, I stopped just outside the kitchen and waited for my heart to stop racing. Standing with her back to me, her hair was in two fat braids, the shorts I'd bought her barely covering her cheeks. She was wearing one of the new halter tops and while I couldn't see her front, I was confident I could make her nipples go from zero to hard in less than a minute. It was a sight I could wake up to for the rest of my life.

Walking up behind her, I snaked my arms around her waist and she leaned into me. When she turned her head to look up, I bent down and took her lower lip between my teeth. She tasted like peppermint, and as I eased my hand inside her shorts, I found a little slice of heaven.

Nibbling my way from her lips to her ear, I stopped long enough to whisper, "You're always wet and ready for me. How do you do that?"

"Do you want the scientific explanation?"

"Will it put me to sleep?"

"Probably."

"Then give me the short version, the one I want to hear."

She turned on tiptoe and put her arms around my neck. "You mean the one where I look at you or smell you or feel your touch and my insides go all liquid and hot?"

"Yeah, that's the one."

She laughed and pushed me away. "Sit down before breakfast gets cold."

I still had a mind to have her for breakfast, that hot little body stretched across the kitchen table, but there was always lunch.

Her version of breakfast was delicious, the best French toast I'd ever had, but as much as she tried to hide it, I knew she was uneasy. The phone call, necessary as it was, put a damper on the morning.

I hated that I had to take her down the road we were headed. It was one thing to know your father was an uncaring bastard, quite another to think he might be capable of your murder. At least during breakfast, I wanted to keep things light so I'd stowed my laptop under the table out of sight.

"Jordan, about tonight."

I reached over and cupped her cheek. "Sweetheart, it's only dinner with my family. There's no reason to be nervous."

"I'm sure that's true and I'm looking forward to it but unless you bought me underwear and have it hidden away, we need to make a trip into town."

I was busted but I took it like a man. "Can I pick it out?"

"Not a prayer, lover boy. These shorts barely cover the naughty bits."

Keeping in mind that it's always important to know your opponent's negotiating strengths, I asked, "What's in it for me?"

She touched her upper lip with that pretty pink tongue of hers and said, "When we get home from dinner, you can take it off with your teeth."

I was intending to do that anyway, along with a few other things she'd never learned in grad school, but I let her think she won that round. "Done. We'll drive in after breakfast."

For a new relationship, the silence that flowed between us was more comfortable than awkward, but I could tell from the way she scrunched up her nose that she was thinking about something.

"Something else on your mind, sweetheart?"

"As a matter of fact, there is. On the beach, you said something about serving at the pleasure of people above my father's pay grade; that he'd snarled at the wrong dogs. What did you mean by that? But please don't tell me if you have to kill me afterwards."

"I'll tell you this much. We all know there's a faction inside and outside the government who likes nothing better than taking us to war. Every time a missile is fired or a country is invaded, someone's pockets are getting lined and it's usually the person who's screaming the loudest about patriotism and national security. Sometimes war is inevitable, no one is contesting that, but sometimes it isn't. There's a group of people dedicated to solving problems before they get to bloodshed. We work for them."

"You mean a secret society like the Bilderbergs or Trilateral Commission?"

"Something like that but those two aren't very secret if you know their names, are they?"

"Did everyone at IIF know this but me?"

"We take it case by case but everyone is on a need-to-know except for a few, a very few."

"The ones you trust. Would you ever have trusted me if someone hadn't tried to kill me or…"

I grinned at her. "Are you trying to pick a fight with me?"

"It depends on whether or not you fight fair."

Hauling her into my lap, I had her face me and straddle my thighs. She was light as a feather and I realized again how tiny she was. She brought out every protective instinct I had and a few I was sure were new. Skimming my fingers inside her top, I cupped a breast that fit my hand like it was made for it, which I suspected it was.

"You don't fight fair at all, do you, Mr. Dunham?"

She squirmed in my lap until her crotch was cradling my cock, already straining to be free. "It seems neither of us plays fair, Dr. Forrest, but don't start something you can't finish. We wouldn't want to wear it out in the first twenty-four hours."

Tracing my beard with the tip of her finger, she finished up by outlining my mouth. "A woman's vaginal walls are very resilient. I'm a scientist, I know these things."

"I wasn't talking about yours."

"Oh, please. I've heard the guys talk. You have quite a reputation with the ladies."

"You know my policy on honesty. Is there something else you want to ask me?"

She shimmied off my lap and took her seat at the table. "There is but it isn't about your sex life. Technically, it's more of a request than a question. I want to be kept in the loop about what you and Dylan discover about my incident."

"Incident? Your car wasn't vandalized, Sydney. It was blown to bits and you were supposed to be in it."

"I realize that but if you care for me…"

"If I care for you?" When she pulled her eyes from mine and looked down at her hands, I knew something was up. "What's this about?"

"You've done a very good job of keeping me occupied so I won't think about things, haven't you?"

Bingo. Under the circumstances, I did a first-rate job of keeping my anger tamped down when what I really wanted to do was drag her back to bed and fuck every doubt from her mind. "If I remember correctly, you knocked on my door last night, not the other way around."

"I did, didn't I?"

Those beautiful eyes filled with tears and I knew the only person I had to protect her from at that moment was herself. The courage it took for her to make that long walk down the hall, to open her heart and give herself to me after all she'd been through was a gift, and not one I took lightly. "Come here, you crazy broad."

Again, she came willingly into my lap and I held her close. "I'll make a deal with you. You never again question my feelings for you and I'll keep you in the loop. Deal?"

"Deal."

I reached down and picked up my laptop. It took a few minutes to boot it up, during which I multi-tasked and felt up every luscious inch of her. When I checked my email, I opened the one from Dylan and Smoke Boy was there in all his glory. Dylan had chosen a frame shot only moments before he approached Sydney and it was remarkably clear. Younger than I originally thought, he looked to be in his early thirties, his clothes nicely-tailored, hair short and expensively-maintained. He was also a good-looking sonofabitch if one liked the blond Adonis type.

Sydney glanced at the screen and back at me, her face expressionless.

"Sweetheart, this is the guy you kicked in the balls. Do you have any idea who he is?"

She closed her eyes and a single tear slipped out. "His name is Jeffrey Stanhope Prentiss III. We were once engaged."

16

It is easier to forgive an enemy than to forgive a friend.
—William Blake

I hadn't intended to blurt it out that way, nor had I intended to get emotional, but seeing Jeff in that photograph, juxtaposing the boy I'd loved with the man I despised made me heartsick.

I felt Jordan's body stiffen and saw the anger in his eyes but neither could be helped. It was what it was.

"You might have mentioned that before, Sydney." His tone was back to one with which I was all too familiar, my inquisitor.

Rising from his lap, I walked several feet away and leaned against a countertop. "When did you want me to mention it, Jordan, on the beach, when we were in bed? Except for Dylan asking me what I remembered of Moonstone Beach, this is the first time we've discussed it."

"It must have been serious between the two of you if you were engaged."

"It was very serious, as serious as anything can be when you're five years old. He was seven. We were playing in my backyard. I was Guinevere and he was Lancelot. He asked me if I'd marry him when we grew up and I said yes. Our parents were good friends and Jeff and I were thrown together from the time I was a baby. He was my only friend and the one person I might have confided in about the rape. My father must have known that because when the rape started, we weren't allowed to play together anymore. His father travelled a lot for his job and my father stepped in to do all the things a father would normally do, at least a Greenwich father. He taught him to play golf, to shoot skeet, to sail.

"Jeff's father was a Harvard man but my father went to Yale so Jeff went to Yale. My father was Skull and Bones so Jeff was Skull and Bones. He became my father's son in every conceivable way, including making me the object of his disdain. When I made the decision to switch from law to a career in forensic science, he came to Vassar and raised hell with me. He said I'd never been anything but a disappointment to my parents, that I should grow up and do what was expected of me and if I toed the line and started cooperating, he'd consider marrying me even though I wasn't suitable wife material. Amanda overheard the conversation and called campus security. He was escorted off-campus and he wasn't happy about it. Prior to the other day in the parking lot, I'd only seen him a couple of times since then, trailing after my father like a puppy dog."

"Is he with the Agency?"

"I'm not sure but I think his involvement with my father is unofficial, like an aide."

"Where does your mother fit into this unholy alliance?"

"My mother hasn't drawn a sober breath in years. I suspect it's the way she copes with being married to him. But I won't judge her, I can't. I don't even know her."

I realized I'd related the whole sordid tale without once looking at Jordan. I didn't have to. I knew what I'd see on his face and that knowledge turned my stomach. I could hear the wheels turning, how best to free himself from this pathetic woman, a woman so unlovable that everyone in her life had eventually shunned her.

A chill crept down my spine. There was a reason Jeff's face was on the computer, a reason we were discussing what happened in the parking lot and not the beach. In Dylan and Jordan's minds the two were connected.

A sound bubbled up from my throat, a mixture of laughter and hysteria. "My God, Jordan, you have lousy taste in women."

Like his reputation with the fairer sex, his temper was legendary but I'd never experienced it until he got up, threw the chair across the room and stomped to within a foot of me. Penning me in place with his hands on the countertop, he was so angry he was shaking. "Now you listen to me, sweetheart, because I'm not going to repeat this ever again. I don't give a fuck that you were raised by wolves. I'm not your asshole father, I'm not the monster who raped you and I'm sure as hell not Pretty Boy Prentiss. I don't know who cooked up that fireworks show but we're going to find out, and when we do, they're going down. No one messes with my woman, physically or emotionally, without paying the price."

He melted me from the inside out and I rested my cheek on his chest. "I love it when you go all caveman on me, but you do realize you sound like a country western song, right?"

His response was a chuckle. "Hell of a way to break an engagement. He's probably still got ice on his balls."

"I miscalculated. I was aiming for his head." He curled a finger under my chin and held it there while he bent down and took my lips in a slow deep kiss, one that was interrupted by the jingle of his cell phone. He seemed inclined to ignore it until I pulled back. "You'd better take that."

"I'd rather take you, right here, right now."

"I'm not going anywhere."

The second he stepped away from me, I felt the loss of his strength, the power in his hard, muscled body and the heat of his embrace. But unlike last time when I left the room, I stayed and listened to Jordan's end of the conversation.

"Smoke Boy's name is Jeffrey Stanhope Prentiss III." He redirected his attention to me and asked, "You have any idea where he's living now?"

I shook my head. "In addition to the house in Greenwich, my parents own a townhouse in Georgetown. I assume Jeff lives somewhere close by."

Jordan gave the information to Dylan while I busied myself clearing the breakfast dishes. I was still grappling with the implication of Jeff and/or my father being complicit in an attempt on my life. Was it possible that two men who had known me from birth would engineer my death? But if not them, then who? Other than my supervisor at Quantico, I'd made more friends than enemies during my time with the Bureau.

When Jordan started speaking again, I put my thoughts on hold.

"...find out how Prentiss returned to D.C. and when. And then we need to shake things up a bit, maybe get him looking over his shoulder. Use that guy at AP and have him leak it that the Feds are looking at a close family friend in the disappearance and attempted murder of the lovely Dr. Forrest. He can cite an anonymous source in the San Luis Obispo detective division."

Dylan was saying something and Jordan glanced my way and winked. I'd heard enough so I left the room to change the bedding and tidy up the bathrooms. The least I could do was earn my keep. It was only a matter of minutes before I heard the television in the great room and went out to investigate.

The cable news channels were all over the bombing of my car, my disappearance the lead story. If there was anything more disconcerting than seeing myself on a fifty-two inch television, I had yet to experience it. It made me feel naked and exposed, far more so than the brief glimpse I had of my performance at *Naughty Nellie's*.

Alerted to my presence in the doorway, Jordan turned off the TV. "We had to expect this, sweetheart. If it's any consolation, you look beautiful."

"Right now, how I look isn't high on my list of priorities." I chose my next words carefully. "Jordan, I think I should go back. I'll tell them I ran because I was frightened. With all the media attention, no one's going to try anything. You can go back to IIF and we'll see one another after hours or I'll go back to work and you can keep an eye on me there. At some point, someone is going to notice that we're both gone and connect the dots. I want you out of the line of fire."

"You bored with me already?"

I leveled him with a look that was half pout, half perturbed. "You're not listening to me."

He called my look and raised me a look, the one where his eyebrow shot up and his lips twitched. "You're right, I'm not."

"Well, you should be. We're having a serious discussion."

"No, you're having a serious discussion and I'm thinking about having an early lunch and how long it will take to get you naked on the bed."

I took a couple of steps back. "I know what you're doing. You're trying to take my mind off things with sex and it's not going to work."

"Wanna bet?"

Then things get a little fuzzy. He was coming toward me and the last thing I remember was thinking it was a good thing I hadn't taken the bet. I would have lost.

17

When that woman set her mind to it, she could move like the wind. She was still pouting but I had plans for dealing with that when we got home from dinner. In the meantime, I took off my shirt but left on my jeans, which seemed to rattle her even more.

"Clothes off, scootch into the middle of the bed and put your hands above your head. And if you know what's good for you, Sunshine, you'll leave them there."

I knew she wanted to protest but her curiosity got the better of her. Her eyes were wide as saucers and she moistened her lips but did exactly as I told her to. Instead of lying down next to her, I sat on the edge of the bed and let my fingers do the walking.

And it was a hell of a stroll, slow and leisurely, like I had all the time in the world. I don't know how long I sat there, the tips of my fingers roaming here and there. I started with that pouty lower lip and worked my way across to her ear and down the side of her neck. Judging from the moan that escaped her, the place where her neck met her shoulder was a particularly good spot and I dallied there a bit. Her nipples were next and I admit to dallying and dawdling just because I could.

"How's the thinking coming, sweetheart? You solve the case yet?"

Her breathing was labored when she unfisted one of her hands and flipped me the bird. If I hadn't already been in love with her, that would have done it. She gave as good as she got and drove me crazy in the process.

By the time I got to her belly button, she was getting kind of fidgety, so before she came without me, I figured it was time to move things along. No way was I getting cheated out of this.

My hand went first, to test the waters so to speak, and she was wet and ready. Spreading her legs, I situated myself between her thighs and cupped her ass. I lapped up her cream like a hungry kitten. I couldn't get enough. She tasted so good, smelled so good I could have feasted there forever. More than once I'd imagined this and like everything else about this woman, it beat the living hell out of my expectations.

"Jordan?"

One glance at her face told me all I needed to know. "Shhh, baby, I'll take care of you."

And I intended to, when I was damn good and ready. When she started writhing beneath me, I lubed my finger in her cream and explored her anus, another thing I had plans for later.

"Please?"

She said the magic word and I sucked her pearly clit. Her climax rolled through her but I was unrelenting. With fingers not otherwise engaged, I invaded her sheath and massaged the taut little bundle of nerves I'd grown to know and love.

"Oh, my God."

If once was good, twice was even better as I felt her inner walls quake and shudder. As the last of the tremors died away, I crawled up next to her and took her in my arms. "Now be a good girl and sleep while I run into town and get you some underwear."

With sleepy eyes, she looked up at me. "You said I could go."

"That was before your photograph was plastered all over the TV. How long do you think it would take before some nosy sales clerk dropped a dime on you?"

"Now you sound like Sam Spade."

Here's the thing about shopping for your woman's underwear after you've spent the last half hour with your face buried in her pussy. Her scent stays with you and the longer you smell her, the tinier the bra and panties you end up buying.

Hence the raucous laughter when she pulled them from the bag. "You've got to be kidding."

"What."

"We're having dinner with your parents, Jordan. I'm not auditioning for *Girls Gone Wild*."

"That's true but unless you're planning on reprising your *Naughty Nellie's* routine as the evening's entertainment, who's going to know? Besides, it's less to chew off when we get home."

She crumpled the bag and threw it at my head. "You're insatiable."

"Damn right. What smells so good?"

"I may have been raised by wolves but even I know you don't go empty-handed to someone's house for dinner. I baked a pie."

As a trained investigator, I should have figured that one out. I assumed what flour wasn't on her face and in her hair was reserved for the crust. "Good for you. Have you ever baked a pie, sweetheart?"

She threw me a look. "I can extract DNA from a sample the size of a pinhead. A pie is nothing more than flour, shortening, water and fruit. How tough can it be?"

"Uh huh." I pulled her into my arms.

Rising to her toes, she rubbed her nose against my chin. "You smell like me."

"Yep, and you smell even better than apples and cinnamon."

During my two-month stint in Bahrain, IIF business had been brisk so I spent most of the afternoon on the computer playing catch-up. We also had a shitload of new cases, and since I had no idea when I'd be returning to the office, I went through them, delegating the urgent ones and putting others on hold. I needed to keep busy. If I let my mind wander to Sydney and the sweet delights of her body, I'd succumb. She was my addiction, pure and simple, and I loved every minute of it.

For her part, she seemed content to putter in the kitchen, walk the property and give me space to work. With her history and recent brush with death, she should have been a basket case. Her calm amazed me. I wanted to believe it was me, that she was comfortable with me, that she trusted me, but I knew deep down it was more than that. She'd been on her own so long, she lived inside her head where it was safe. Intellectually I got it but the male in me, the ego part, balked at the idea. I wanted all of her, not just her body.

Before we went to dinner, my plan was to get her in the shower for some soapy one-on-one, but she beat me to the punch and took a bath. By the time I was ready, she was dressed and waiting in the great room, her attention focused on the TV. She looked beautiful as always but there was an expression on her face I couldn't read, one I hadn't seen, one I hoped to never see again. It broke my fucking heart.

Standing before a bank of microphones, eyes concealed behind oversized sunglasses, Helena Forrest was attempting to stay upright, her arm linked through her husband's. Beside her, Deputy Director Roger Forrest was fielding questions from a slew of reporters, his voice somber. "Our only child is missing, our precious daughter. How do you think we feel?" He pointed to a woman in front.

"Deputy Director Forrest, it's no secret that you're planning to make a run for the Senate in 2012. Assuming Sydney's returned unharmed, will her disappearance have any effect on your decision?"

"I'm not sure I understand the question, Joanne."

"When Governor Burrows' son was kidnapped, he made the decision to keep his family out of the limelight and declined to run for another term. Is that something you'd consider?"

Forrest was shaking his head. "Sydney wouldn't want that. In our telephone conversation last Sunday, she said, 'The country needs you, Daddy. Please don't ever let anything or anyone dissuade you from running.' I think that says it all. Now if you'll excuse us…"

"One more question, sir. It's been reported that the FBI is looking at a family friend, Jeffrey Prentiss, as a person of interest in connection with the attempt on your daughter's life and subsequent disappearance. Would you care to comment?"

Either he hadn't anticipated the question or knew nothing of recent developments, but his well-practiced composure slipped as did his wife's. When she almost nosedived off the platform, I wanted to kiss that reporter. Forrest was the first to recover and I noticed his voice was tighter but still reeked of paternal pathos.

"I would hardly consider him a friend but I want to take this opportunity to ask him to come forward and account for his whereabouts. And so help me God, if it is determined that he is responsible in any way, I will personally see that he is punished to the full extent of the law."

The only thing missing at the end of his diatribe was a wink and I would have given anything to know what was going through his head.

Sydney pointed the remote at the television and turned it off. I realized she hadn't seen me standing in the doorway and for once I kept my trap shut and observed. Stepping onto the deck, she leaned into the railing and gazed out at the lake.

Torn between giving her *space* and rendering comfort, I walked out right behind her but kept my distance. "You okay, sweetheart?"

She didn't answer me at first, just nodded. After a few minutes, she took a deep breath. "When I first started at the Bureau, my father called and asked me to attend a party, some Agency thing. He said it was important to him, that my absence would reflect badly on him. I went and played the loving daughter as he wanted me to. I had no intention of spending the night at their townhouse in Georgetown but it snowed and I couldn't get home. Before I left the next morning, I snuck into their bathroom and took his hairbrush and a tube of her lipstick. When I got back to the lab, the first thing I did was test our DNA, all the while praying they weren't my real parents, that I'd been dropped on their doorstep by gypsies. No such luck."

"We have no control over who we get as parents, sweetheart, but at some point we have to talk about the sexual abuse thing, how you're coping with it and what I can do to help."

"It's not a *thing*, Jordan. It's part of who I am and I've dealt with it all my life. It's not an issue."

She was shutting me out and all I could hear were Dylan's words rattling around in my head. *Depending on how much therapy she's had to get past the sexual abuse, it may or may not come back to bite both of you in the ass.*

"It didn't sound that way last night."

Her smile was playful and just a tad naughty. "Yes, but you fixed me, didn't you?"

I wasn't fooled for a second. Two things were obvious. I was being stroked and the subject would come up again. My only hope was for resolution before someone got their butt chomped.

18

No one forgives with more grace and love than a child.
—*Gordon Atkinson, Real Live Preacher*

Before I could fasten my seatbelt, Jordan reached over and did it for me, brushing my lips with a kiss. I wasn't sure if it was motivated by genuine affection or concern that I'd jump from the car and go screaming through the woods.

Whatever the reason, I loved him for it. "Stop worrying about me, I'm fine."

And I was, for the most part. My parents' performance was neither more nor less than I expected. Their theatrics weren't new, nor was their callous disregard for my safety. I was their wind-up toy, the thing they pulled out, dusted off and wound up to suit their needs.

His hand found mine and gave a squeeze. "You're not

worried about meeting my family, are you?"

I glanced down at the foil-covered dish in my lap. What was I thinking? "No, I'm worried they'll eat my pie and die."

His glance at my lap was involuntary but I noticed he blanched.

"That was a joke, Jordan. I'm trying to lighten the mood. Work with me here."

"Fair enough. What do you call a lesbian with training wheels on her motorcycle?"

I rolled my eyes. "The guys at IIF laid that one on me my first week."

He seemed surprised. "Did they give you a hard time?"

"No, they were great, really great. Thank God in this day and age everyone knows someone who's gay."

"I never really believed it, you know. I always knew you were straight."

"Of course you did, love, you being a trained investigator and all."

By the time we arrived at his parents' home, I wasn't nervous, I was petrified. What if they hated me on sight? What if they were deeply religious and believed all scientists were the spawn of Satan? What if they thought Jordan should jump the next plane and get away from the crazy woman whom someone was trying to kill?

"Breathe, sweetheart. They're going to love you."

I blinked from my reverie and returned his smile. *Not if I poison them.*

The house was beautiful, triple the size of Jordan's and closer to the lake. Surrounded on four sides by an ornate iron wall, it was also secure. But I liked his better, perhaps because his imprint was on it. Or perhaps because the only love I'd ever known, the only love I wanted to know, I'd found there.

The interior of the house was just as lovely, as were the people who welcomed me. I could see where Jordan got his looks. Somewhere in their sixties, his parents were striking.

His father, John, leaned in and kissed me on the cheek and Emily, his mother, embraced me. "You're just as beautiful as J.D. said you were, Sydney. Welcome to our home."

I felt a tug on my hand and looked down. A little boy was staring up at me. Lowering myself to sit on my heels, I asked, "And who are you?"

Emily stepped forward and ruffed the little boy's hair. "This is Joshua, our grandson. Jennifer and her husband and Jamie, our youngest, are running late as usual."

I redirected my attention to Joshua. "How old are you, sweetheart?"

"I'm five. Can I touch your hair?"

"Sure you can." No matter what I did with my hair, it was always a mess, but children seemed to love it, why I don't know. Removing the scrunchie that kept it in place at the nape of my neck, I shook my head and let it fly free.

"I like it. It's soft and smells good."

Jordan grabbed Joshua in a bear hug and tossed him over his shoulder. "Get your own girl, Sport, that one's mine."

That one's mine. His words brought a tingle to my tummy and I stood up just in time to see a look pass between Jordan's parents. They were beaming.

Still holding the pie, I bit the bullet and offered it to Emily. "I had some time on my hands today so I baked a pie, but please don't hold it against me if it's awful."

Laughing, Jordan put his free arm around my shoulders. "Way to sell it, sweetheart."

As if on cue, my father's voice stole the moment and I jumped. When I found my breath, I glanced toward the adjoining room where an enormous TV hung suspended on a wall. *"Our precious daughter. . . "*

John Dunham took one look at my face and bolted for the great room. "I think we can do without that."

The awkwardness of the moment was saved by Emily as she crooked her arm in mine. "Come with me, Sydney. I'll give you a tour of the house and we can make our way to the kitchen for some girl talk and tea."

Jordan groaned. "That sounds like trouble. I've spent the last two days convincing her I'm perfect."

She reached up and patted his cheek. "I seriously doubt that, dear."

As promised, we wound up in the kitchen and Emily wasted

no time in getting down to the reason she'd sequestered me. When we were seated at the kitchen table, she looked down at her hands and not at me. Shifting in the chair, I prepared for the worst.

"Sydney, we're a very close-knit family and a relatively happy one compared to most. John and I have always tried to instill in our children a love of life and an appreciation for everything it offers. Believe it or not, the one we've worried about the most, even over our two daughters, is J.D."

The ball was in my court but I wasn't sure what to do with it. "He's an amazing man, Emily. He's kind and..."

"Are you in love with him? I know I must sound like the worst kind of meddlesome mother but I haven't seen him this happy in more years than I can remember. I don't want to see him hurt again."

This time I was the one who avoided eye contact. "I love him very much but..."

"Sydney, he stopped by today on his way back from town and told us about your estrangement from your family. The reasons aren't important and he didn't offer and we didn't ask. But I know something about being on your own with no family to fall back on, feeling adrift and somehow unworthy of the happiness you're entitled to."

Despite my best efforts, I hadn't fooled anyone, least of all myself. Other than taking precaution that I wouldn't get pregnant, Jordan hadn't mentioned marriage, and I had no reason to believe he would. Still, the idea that I might someday have children and be like my parents, detached and disengaged, frightened me to death. "Is it that obvious?"

"Only to one who's been there." The water was boiling and Emily rose from her chair to prepare our tea. "My parents were both abusive alcoholics. I was sixteen when I boarded a bus in San Diego and ran away from home. I'd stolen just enough money from my mother's purse to get me as far as San Luis Obispo. The only thing I knew about the town was from school when we studied Father Serra and the mission, so when I got off the bus, I found my way there. The things I did on the street no child should ever have to do. But every morning, I went to the mission and sat there for hours, praying for a miracle. And then one Sunday, the Dunham family went to mass there. I always sat in the back pew and I'd noticed them. They were so clean and nice to one another. I had no idea they'd seen me but on their way out that day, John's father stopped at my pew and put his hand out to me. He never said a word and I still don't know how I knew to take it, but I did. I took his hand and he led me out with the rest of his family. When we got to their house, he showed me to a room and told me what time lunch was being served and that we'd talk later. I never left. Six years later, John and I were married and a year after that J.D. was born. We named him Jordan after John's father."

I was touched she had shared so much with me, but there

was something I needed to know. "Did Jordan ask you to speak with me?"

"My children don't know about my past, Sydney. They think I met the Dunhams when I worked their vineyard one summer."

"But you don't know me, Emily. It's not that I'm ungrateful but how can you share something so intimate and private with a total stranger?"

"I know my son." She took my hand. "John's father told me something that first day that I've never forgotten. He said that every day we wake up and make a conscious decision to be who and what we are. My parents did that and yours do too. It's all about choices, dear. We are the sum total of the choices we make about how to live our lives." She nodded toward the great room. "Don't let their poor choices influence yours. Forgive them and go on with your life."

Voices from the foyer drew our attention and we knew our girl talk was over. "Thank you, Emily. I needed this, more than you'll ever know."

I started to follow her out of the kitchen and meet the rest of the family when Jordan appeared out of nowhere, took my arm and steered me down the hall. Inside a powder room, he closed the door and locked it. Not that I wanted to, but before I could protest, I was sitting atop the pedestal sink. I giggled, all the while trying to keep him at arms' length. "What are you doing? Your family's here."

He was getting very proficient at keeping me quiet by kissing me and this time was no exception. Taking my lips softly at first, his tongue did wicked things with mine and I felt my arousal dampen what little fabric there was between my legs.

Clever man that he was, he knew it too. "Spread your legs, straddle the sink and put your hands behind you near the faucets. If you move and send me out of here with a hard-on, you'll pay for it later."

Always up for a challenge, I rubbed my knee against his groin as I was getting in position. "Oops."

His eyes narrowed and his nostrils flared. "That's going to cost you."

In the length of a heartbeat, his hand was under my skirt, his finger exploring the skin beneath the thin strip of thong. "Baby, you're wet. Do you know how easy it would be to make you come?"

I nodded and closed my eyes, desperate for him to do something. "You planned this whole thing, didn't you?"

"I'm a planner. Get use to it."

Readjusting my clothes, he tucked some errant hair behind my ear and lifted me down. He patted me on the butt before he shooed me out the door, but when I looked behind me, I heard the distinct click of the lock.

Rounding the corner to the foyer, I spotted Joshua and lowered myself to his ear. "Your Uncle J.D. is in the powder bath. Why don't you go knock on the door until he comes out?"

He gave me a big toothy smile and took off. Two could play at that game.

The rest of the family was just as warm and welcoming as their parents and put me immediately at ease.

Thankfully, dinner conversation centered on Jordan's two sisters and brother-in-law, all of whom worked for one casino or another in either security or accounting. I had no idea what went on behind the scenes of a casino and was delighted by their stories. By the time the conversation got around to me, I was relaxed.

Jamie, Jordan's younger sister, opened the discussion with a question I was expecting, one I'd often been asked. "Spill it, Sydney. Is a forensics lab as exciting as they make it appear on TV?"

"Absolutely, with the exception of the great lighting, the bells and whistles and the hunky guys." I looked at Jordan and amended my description. "Well, maybe one or two hunky guys."

Everyone laughed except Jordan who spent the better part of dinner staring at me across the table, his intent clear, to have me squirming in my seat. Later tonight I would pay for my transgressions. I couldn't wait.

Leaning back in his chair, John surprised me with a question. "I think I read somewhere that the French were the first to use forensics in police work. Is that true?"

The history of forensic science was a subject near and dear to my heart and I warmed to the subject immediately. "A man by the name of Eugene François Vidocq established the first detective force, the Sûreté of Paris, in the early 1800s but the Chinese actually used fingerprints to establish identity in the eighth century."

The discussion that ensued was lively and animated and I enjoyed myself immensely. By the time dessert was served, I was convinced I'd be forgiven should anyone fall ill.

Joshua, a perfect little gentleman during dinner, climbed down from his chair and walked over to stand by his mother. When he began sniffling and rubbing his eyes, she pulled him onto her lap. "What's wrong, sweetheart?"

"I don't want Uncle J.D. to spank Sydney. I like her."

My face beet red, I shot daggers at Jordan. "Honey, why would you think that?"

"Because he looks like Peter's mommy right before she spanks him."

Ignoring the titters around the table, I attempted to be the voice of reason. "You must be mistaken, sweetheart. Uncle J.D. wouldn't do that."

"Don't bet the farm on that one, sweet cheeks." All eyes flew to Jordan as he dug into his pie. When he finished chewing, he winked at me. "Great pie, by the way."

19

I suppose if I asked most people to describe me, words like asshole and prick would spring to mind. They wouldn't be wrong. I'm quick to lose my temper, always was, and I want what I want when I want it, always will. But my natural tendencies toward dominance spiked considerably with Sydney. They had from the beginning.

Although I wasn't committed to the BDSM lifestyle as a full time thing, I'll admit I dabbled from time to time, even went through the training. The Trident, one of California's most exclusive fetish clubs, was in the area and Dylan and I joined years ago. It was someplace to go on a Saturday night, meet up with like-minded friends and maybe play a scene with a willing sub. No harm, no foul.

For the most part, I preferred vanilla sex, the give and take and surprises. The exception was Sydney. There was something about her that pushed my buttons, a need to possess her, to be the be all and end all of her existence.

It was a risk, especially with her past. Then again, the signs were there, subtle things like a quickening of her pulse when I snapped a command, the dilation of her pupils when I threatened to spank her. She wasn't a submissive, far from it, but she had needs beyond the average woman. And I was just the guy to meet them.

Dinner with my family was great and I knew she enjoyed herself. Now it was my turn. I couldn't wait to get her home, to strip her and slip inside her wet warmth. In the close confines of the car, her scent wrapped around me, intoxicated me, and the need to touch her drove me nuts. I resisted, knowing when I finally did connect with her, the wait would be worth it. Nearing the house, I felt compelled to ratchet up the tension.

"When we get home, run a tub and wait for me in the bathroom." My tone was deliberately clipped, fair warning that it wasn't a request.

Her eyes flew open and I heard her catch a breath.

"Is there a problem?"

Her response was to stare straight ahead and clasp her hands in her lap. Goddamn, she was cute.

By the time I'd secured the house and stripped down to

sweatpants, I was running on borrowed time. I was rock-hard and my balls ached. It didn't help that when I walked into the bathroom, the space was lit by candles, the image surreal. Naked as the day she was born, she was sitting on the edge of the tub trailing her fingers through the water. Her hair was loose and wild and I itched to get my hands in it. She looked innocent and waif-like, completely lost in thought.

"It's true, isn't it? You belong to that club."

There was no censure in her tone, more curiosity than anything else, but the warning bells went off. Rather than approaching her, I leaned against the doorframe. "What club is that?"

"I need to know the rules, Jordan."

"We'll take them as they come. All you have to do is…"

She shook her head. "I know the rules for Dominance and submission, at least some of them. I'm talking about the double standard. It seems I'm the only one in this relationship who's expected to come clean about her past."

She had a point but I wasn't ready to concede it. What I was more than prepared to do was turn her upside down and inside out. "So you think you know the rules for D/s, do you?"

Standing, she grabbed a towel from the side of the tub. When she'd wrapped it around herself and hidden all the goodies, she glared at me. "You're doing it again, not taking me seriously. When you're ready to talk and not answer my question with a question, let me know."

She tried to leave the bathroom but I blocked the door. The towel came off with a flick of my wrist. "Don't test me, baby. One way or another, you're going to wind up in the tub and in my bed."

Her nipples were taut little buds and without the scent of the candles, I was sure I'd smell her arousal, her pussy drenched and needy. She didn't move a muscle. While I gave her points for stubbornness, I was nearing the breaking point, the place where *safe, sane* and *consensual* got kicked to the curb. "Tub. Now."

I detected a hint of a smile, part playful, part challenge, as her hand reached out and wrapped around my cock. "Will you tell me about the club?"

I had to hand it to her, her negotiating skills were improving. Raking the hair back from her face, I held her head in place and did it again, answered her question with a question. "Now that you've got it, what are you doing to do with it?"

Her eyes were fixed on mine as her hands went to the waistband of my sweatpants. Careful to ease them over my dick, she drew them down and dropped to her knees. Tentative at first, her tongue reached out to snag a drop of fluid. I watched, fascinated, as she worked through the mechanics of her first blow job. Licking me from root to head, she took her time exploring, nipping and nibbling until she drew me into the hot, wet cavern of her mouth. She took me deep, sucking and hollowing her cheeks until I thought I'd lose my mind. She was a natural.

I knew I wouldn't last, not a chance in hell, and I wasn't ready to come. With more machismo than brains, I pulled gently from her mouth and scooped her up.

"Fuck the bath."

20

Love is an act of forgiveness, a tender look which becomes a habit.
—Peter Ustinov

I suppressed a nervous giggle as he plucked me from the floor and turned toward the bedroom. From the set of his jaw, I deduced he was about to make good on his promise, the one that assured my butt would pay the price for my behavior.

Attempting to soften the blow, I looped my arms around his neck and nipped his earlobe. "Sweetheart?"

The endearment hadn't quite left my lips when I was laid facedown across his thighs, his enraged cock bobbing at my hip. The first slap took me by surprise and I yelped, while the second hurt like hell. Clearly, he was no novice at the punishment thing, a fact I didn't wish to dwell on. After long, tear-filled minutes, the pain became pleasure and I moaned.

When the spanking stopped, he caressed my ass, but by then I was drifting. His murmured words calmed me, soothed my brain as my body craved more.

Still draped over his lap, I felt his fingers slip between my sopping folds. "Hmm, somebody likes to be spanked." The tip of his finger touched my clit and I reached for release, every nerve ending poised. "Not yet, baby, relax." The lube was cold and I jumped. Gentling me, he spread the cheeks of my ass and prepared my virgin hole.

Getting there is half the fun. Those words became my mantra as his finger invaded the first tight ring of muscle. After a moment, the burning subsided and I went with the sensations thrumming through my core. I held off as long as I could but when the plug was seated and his thumb caressed my clit, I lost myself to wave upon wave of pulsing pleasure.

I had mere seconds to recover when I was lifted and settled on the bed. Before me on his knees, Jordan spread my legs and left a trail of kisses from my tummy to my breasts, licking them, loving them, as only he could do. Despite having just come, I was dizzy with excitement, so aroused I couldn't breathe. His scent, the feel of his skin and the desire in his eyes drove me to heights I'd only imagined. When the head of his cock breached the entrance to my sheath, I heard myself moaning, whimpering my pleas for him to fuck me.

And he did, slowly and completely. Wanton was not a word I would have ascribed to myself but I was all of that and more. His tenderness touched me, the way he took his time to ensure my enjoyment. But it was his control, the low, guttural way he spoke that stoked my fire.

"Don't move. Just feel my cock gliding into you. Feel your muscles embrace it, your juices bathe it. Feel the plug, how it fills you, and imagine my cock in its place. You're mine, Sydney. Every breath you take, every groan of passion, every orgasm belongs to me."

His tongue came down to duel with mine and I climbed higher still. It was all too much. My body was a clutching mass of need and he my provider. With a final stroke, his head flew back, his neck muscles strained to the breaking point. Through gritted teeth, he ordered me to come.

Gasping for air, I let the maelstrom take me, rock me, rip me apart. Molten lava sluiced through my core, searing everything it touched. When our shudders finally ebbed, he rolled to his side and pulled me to him, his lips brushing my temple.

"Damn, honey, you're going to kill me."

"What would be the fun in that?" I tried to sound chipper but my emotions were in chaos. A trickle of unease, unbidden and unwanted, made itself known but the reason eluded me. Perhaps I was afraid that when the danger passed I would be back on my own, that this was just an interlude for him. Or perhaps it was something else, something I didn't want to look at, a niggling suspicion that I was in over my head.

Loosening his hold on me, he crooked his elbow and rested his cheek on his hand. "Marry me. We'll drive to Vegas tomorrow and find one of those tacky chapels with an Elvis impersonator."

My first thoughts were *how very Jordan*. He'd sensed my disquiet and was trying to joke me out of it. Giving his mouth a loud, sloppy kiss, I wriggled from his grasp and slid from the bed. "Anyone but Elvis. Get me Bon Jovi or Springsteen and I'm in."

Halfway to the bathroom, I was brought up short by the edge to his voice. "Is that a no?"

The air left my lungs in a whoosh. "You're serious?"

"As serious as a heart attack which I might just have if you don't come back to bed and talk to me."

He patted the mattress but I stayed rooted to the spot, knowing the next few minutes could well dictate our future. "We hardly know one another, Jordan."

"I know everything I need to know about you, Sydney, and the rest we'll find out over time."

The anxiety was back but now it had a name. Fear. Jordan's interest in domination came as no surprise. Contrary to the accepted wisdom, men gossiped as much as women, and during my tenure at IIF I'd been privy to more than one whispered conversation about his tastes, Dylan's too. Curious and infatuated, part of me had hoped it was true, that I would be the one to meet his needs. What I hadn't considered is that at some point we'd have to get out of bed. Silly me.

Now I had doubts. Faced with a lifetime commitment, I wasn't sure I could handle it. A little harmless play was one thing but the prospect of repeating a pattern and living under the thumb of another dominant male, no matter how much I loved him, frightened me to death.

"I'm not part of your world, Jordan."

"My world? Is this about the club?" Shaking his head, he leapt from the bed. "It's something I do, Sydney, not who I am."

The smile on his face got my back up and I snarled, "Oh, really? Well, if it's no big deal, why am I the only one in this room with a plug up her ass?"

His laughter filled the room as he stalked toward me, backing me into a wall. "Sweetheart, if I were inclined to want to live the D/s lifestyle, which I am not, right now you'd be in so much trouble it would take an act of congress to get you out of it." He picked me up and held me against the wall, his large hands cupping my poor inflamed butt. "Now, let's try this again. Sydney Forrest, *you* are my world. I love everything about you, your beauty, your brains and your sass. I'm offering you a lifetime to straighten out my kinks. What do you say?"

What could I say? As hard as I might fight it, The Prince of Darkness held my heart and body in thrall. "I say yes, on one condition."

"What's that?"

"We save a couple of kinks, you know, in case I get bored."

21

I knew better than most that marriage offered no guarantees, but I could promise with impunity that boredom would be the least of her problems. She would be loved and cherished but never bored, especially in bed. It was my personal mission.

I lost count of the number of times we reached for one another through the night. We were like kids, the bed our playground. We tussled, tickled and explored, each time sweeter than the last.

Managing to sleep through the alarm, it was almost ten when I woke up. Sydney was curled next to me and gave a soft moan of contentment before burrowing in closer, dead to the world. Had I not had things to do before we left for Vegas, nothing short of a hydrogen bomb could have wrenched me from her arms.

With as much stealth as I could muster, I slipped from the bed and showered in the guest bath so as not to awaken her. A few toiletries and a change of clothes thrown into an overnight bag and I was ready for the eight-hour drive.

Dylan was first up on my list. After making a pot of coffee, I sat down in the kitchen to call him, to advise him of our plans and get the latest scoop on Smoke Boy's whereabouts. Believing himself to be a person of interest in Sydney's disappearance, the odds favored Prentiss going underground or leaving the country. As it turned out, he'd chosen the latter. After dropping Forrest off at SLO airport, Prentiss had driven to Phoenix and flown non-stop to El Paso, just over the border from Juarez. That Dylan was able to track his movements with a few well-placed phone calls while the Feds were still chasing their own asses was hardly a surprise.

Although we had friends in high places, we had something even better, friends in low places, a couple of El Paso's grungiest undercover narcs who owed us a favor, no questions asked. They had some downtime coming and were more than happy to go off the grid, earn some extra cash and nose around south of the border. It was an easy gig. In a place like Juarez, Prentiss' Ivy League looks would stand out like a hooker at a prayer meeting, and with any luck he'd wind up busted or dead. Whichever way it went was fine by me.

144

That the Feds hadn't shown up at IIF was another no-brainer and I could see Forrest's beefy hand in that. Guilty or not, his worst nightmare would be some officious asshole nosing around in our office and discovering the tape of his *Father of the Year* performance. There was no love lost between the Bureau and the Agency so I wasn't sure how he'd managed it. I was only glad he did. Add to that the fact that I hadn't been tagged with a *person of interest* moniker, and the guy deserved a fruit basket. Right after I kicked his ass.

In my mind, I was debating whether or not to tell Sydney of Smoke Boy's defection when Dylan anticipated me and threw in his two cents. "It's up to you how much to tell our girl but my advice is to keep things on the down-low until we know more."

So much for keeping her in the loop but I had to agree with him. I was a selfish prick. I wanted her attention on me and not the fuckwad who'd tried to kill her. "I agree. By the way, if you're not doing anything tonight, how about flying to Vegas and joining us for dinner? You can be our witness tomorrow."

His laughter damn near punctured my eardrum. "Christ, amigo, you move fast. I'm envious as hell but I wouldn't miss it. You sure you don't want me to fly into Tahoe and pick you two up? That's a long goddamn drive."

Speaking of the she-devil, I smelled her body wash about the time I felt her arms encircle my neck.

"I appreciate the offer but eight hours in a car with her naked body sprawled next to me sounds pretty good."

She leaned down, brushed her cheek against mine and whispered, "That better be Dylan."

I hit the speakerphone button and Dylan's voice came through loud and clear.

"It's me, sweetheart. Congratulations. I couldn't be happier you're going to make an honest man of that old reprobate. Sure I can't talk you into marrying me instead?"

"Ah, you're sweet. Maybe next time around."

"Next time around, my ass." I cupped her butt cheek and wiggled my eyebrows when I saw what she was wearing, or not wearing as the case may be, a t-shirt of mine and nothing else.

Her eyes brimmed with mischief as she threw a leg over my lap and straddled me, her body still warm from the shower. If I had to guess, I'd say she was looking to get dirty again. Assuring Dylan I'd call him back, I had just enough time to take a breath before she popped the top button on my jeans.

Palming her breasts beneath the shirt, I let my senses drink their fill. "Something you need, baby woman?"

She made her pissy-face. "Tell you what, big guy. You agree never to call me baby woman again and I won't snip off your balls with my cuticle scissors. Okey dokey?"

I rasped my thumbs over her nipples, loving the feel of them, the way they hardened and puckered at my touch. "Then I suppose *little sub* is off the table too."

"Only if you ever want to have sex with me again."

Sexy and snarky was a potent combination on most women, but Sydney took it to a whole new level. She gave off these little sparks that went straight to my brain and headed south. She knew it too, the little minx. Crossing her arms, she grabbed the hem of the t-shirt and drew it over her head, baring her breasts for my tongue.

I'd created a monster, a copper-haired sex kitten who, at the moment, was pawing through my jeans to reach my dick. And she was wet. Sweet Jesus was she wet. "Whoa, baby. Not that I'm complaining, but do you have a plan here or are you winging it?"

Her response came out as a pant. "Winging it."

It was obvious this form of sexual euphoria precluded speech because that's all I got out of her. Resorting to hand signals, she wrestled my jeans to the floor and commenced riding me like the hounds of hell were on her heels.

The waterworks started when she climaxed, big fat tears that rolled off her cheeks in waves. Bullets and bombs I could deal with but tears scared the piss out of me, especially those brought on by bone-melting sex.

My cock still ensconced in her pussy, I pulled her close and mentally sifted through the things that could be wrong. The spanking? Trident? Marriage? When the blood froze in my veins at the last possibility, I lifted her chin and asked her point blank, "Honey, what's wrong?"

Sniffling once, she looked at me as if I'd lost my freaking mind. "Nothing's wrong, you big jerk, I'm just happy."

And as my blood started pumping again, I thought of my dad and the words he'd etched into the slab of wood that hung in his workshop, the place he'd escape to when my mom and sisters drove him nuts. When the vineyard was sold, he left thousands of dollars' worth of tools but took the sign. Smart guy, my old man.

Women. You know they're gonna kill you. The best you can hope for is to pick the time and place.

World, meet Jordan Dunham. Dead Man Walking.

22

The weak can never forgive.
Forgiveness is the attribute of the strong.
—Mahatma Gandhi

Poor baby. A few post-coital tears and my big, tough superhero folded like an origami crane, a trick I filed away for future use.

I'm not sure what came over me or why I felt compelled to ravish him, but from the moment I woke up, I wanted him inside me. Perhaps it was the need to affirm that he was real, that *we* were real. Whatever the reason, the tears were part of my release, a cleansing, nothing more.

Nor was our journey to Sin City free of drama. An hour out of Tahoe, I panicked. While I knew next to nothing about Nevada marriage licenses, I was fairly certain I'd need some form of I.D., and since I'd locked all mine in the trunk of my Fiat that day at Moonstone Beach, it was either lost in the explosion or drifting on the tide, by now halfway to Honolulu.

And then I remembered my passport. Tucked inside my desk at IIF, it was one of the things I'd planned to retrieve when I went back. A quick phone call to Dylan, a high-five for my handsome chauffeur and we were back in business.

Lulled by the motion of the car, by the third hour I was dozing, that pleasant not-quite-sleep place where the body is safe and the mind is free to float. Predictably, my thoughts went to my father, how incensed he would be at my marriage, and to Jeff, the man he'd become and the man he might have been. But mostly I pondered my future with Jordan, the man who held my hand for no other reason than to let me know he loved me, the man who had saved me from myself.

Still, a million questions bubbled up in my mind. Where would we live? Would he want children right away? Would there be a place for me at IIF? With each new question, I was reminded how little I knew him. But with each mile, each smile of reassurance, I was reminded how little it mattered. Had I known him three years instead of three days, I could not have loved him more. For today at least, I was happy. Tomorrow would take care of itself.

Everything I knew about Las Vegas was gleaned from TV shows or movies. That it would be bright and noisy was a given. Even so, I was unprepared for my first view of Las Vegas Blvd., a major thoroughfare where the sublime embraced the absurd, where decades-old decay was systematically sacrificed to the God of Decadence.

It was close to eight p.m. when we arrived but it could have been midday. The streets teemed with people, tourists and panhandlers, hucksters of every size, shape and color. Lowering the window for a closer look, I heard Jordan laugh.

"It's Vegas, baby."

Music reached my ears and I jerked my head in time to see a brilliant water display light the night. In the background, a luxury hotel loomed high and handsome. "Wow."

"We're home, sweetheart, at least for the next few days."

"We're staying at the Bellagio?"

"Take a good look around because if I have my way, you won't be seeing much besides the inside of the hotel room." His evil grin made my heart race.

"Promises, promises."

"Give me an hour to grab a hot shower and some food and then look out, the evening's young." He took my hand and pressed it to his lips. "I know this probably won't be the wedding of your dreams but when this mess is over we'll have a big, splashy ceremony if you want it, a real honeymoon too."

Releasing the seat belt, I snuggled into him. "I'm not really a big, splashy wedding kind of girl but if you think it will make your mother happy, I'm game."

"You heard her when we told her we were eloping. I don't think she could be any happier. Now the honeymoon on the other hand…"

"Is anywhere you are, my love."

He kissed the top of my head. "You are so going to get lucky tonight."

Obsessed with protecting my anonymity, Jordan had insisted we stop along the way and pick up sunglasses and a funky straw hat to cover my hair. With my face still front and center on the news, one couldn't be too careful, he'd admonished with a frown. At the time I didn't get it. With everything to see and do in Vegas, why would anyone be looking at me?

Of course, he was right. While the tourists might be preoccupied with the bright lights and noise, the surveillance cameras were single-minded in their quest to capture everyone, the good, the bad and the indifferent. And where there were cameras, there was security personnel, hundreds of men and women whose job it was to sit before a bank of screens and monitor the comings and goings of the masses. With the possibility looming that one of them could get lucky, identify me and call my father, it was better to be cautious.

By prearrangement, Dylan met our arrival and hustled us into an elevator, but the big surprise was where he took us. Preceding us by several hours, he'd taken it upon himself to ensure our every comfort with a lavish penthouse suite. As fairy godmothers went, he was the best.

When I jumped into his arms to thank him, he smiled. "I figured you probably wouldn't see much of Vegas except the hotel room so I decided to make it memorable. Everything's on me, including a late supper I ordered up when you called me from downstairs. It should be here any time." He looked over my head toward Jordan. "I'm going to hit the casino and then call it a day. I wrote down my room number on the tablet on the desk."

There was something in his tone that seemed off, but I didn't know him well enough to call him on it. To my shame, I even tried pouting. "You're leaving? We just got here."

The smile he laid on me never touched his eyes. They looked sad. Just when I thought I'd lost the argument, he surprised me again, this time by chucking me under the chin. "You're a handful, aren't you?"

"He's staying."

Jordan's voice was tight, not the easygoing patter I was use to hearing between them; but since my practical experience with men was limited, I figured the undercurrent I'd detected was a *guy* thing. Before I could figure it out, he pulled me to him.

"Speaking of wedding presents, you have one coming from me. What's it going to be, a new car? Whatever you want, just name it."

"The only thing I want right now is a hot shower and to climb into one of those sinfully fluffy bathrobes I saw in the bathroom."

"That works." He put his lips to my ear and whispered,

"Until I can climb into you." Turning me toward the bedroom, he patted my butt. "Now go. The sooner you get clean, the sooner I can get you dirty."

Some of the warmth was back in his voice but I wasn't fooled for a minute. I was being dismissed so the grown-ups could talk. Was this my life now, banishment with bribes of gifts and sex? The pangs resurfaced from the night before but I pushed them down. Road-weary and hungry, I was not in the best shape to take a stand. And tomorrow was another day.

My wedding day.

23

"If that's your idea of a game face, you'd better stay away from the poker tables."

I was pissed, more at myself than Dylan. I'd handled that scene like a rookie, and the only thing I hoped was that Sydney hadn't noticed. Last night's discussion still haunted me, how close I'd come to losing her.

I'm not part of your world, Jordan. The fact that she was referring to the club wasn't the point. I'd promised to keep her in the loop and I was shutting her out. It didn't matter that it was done for all the right reasons, to protect her and spare her further pain. There was a big chunk of my professional world she'd never be part of, not if I could help it.

While Dylan headed for the liquor cart, I collapsed on the sofa. "Talk to me."

He handed me a Scotch and folded himself into a chair. "They found Prentiss. I got the call about an hour ago. I didn't want to call you while you were driving on the off-chance that she'd hear me."

"That was quick. Where'd they find him?"

He took a long pull at his drink and then looked at me. "They found his head in Juarez, the rest of him in El Paso."

I washed the bile down with Scotch. "Christ, don't people just shoot each other anymore? What's with all the sawing and hacking?" I put my hand up. "That was a rhetorical question. Spare me the psychological explanation."

"It's fairly typical for a drug-related hit, J.D."

"Or someone wanted it to look that way, someone who needed to clean up a loose end. And if that's the case, we've got a madman on our hands."

"A madman who wields a lot of power."

A sense of unease settled deep in my bones. Forrest was behind Prentiss's death, I was sure of it. If he could do that to someone as close to him as a son, he'd have no compunction about ordering a similar fate for the child he'd thrown to the dogs. "There's no way to keep this from her, but I'd like to spare her as long as we can, at least until after the wedding."

"Hell of way to start married life."

We'd known one another a long time, Dylan and I. We'd shared everything since we were kids, our dreams, our fears, even some women, but I don't think I'd ever seen him angrier than he was at that moment. It was just a guess, but I doubted it had anything to do with Prentiss.

"There's more, J.D. You've been talking for months about making a few changes to your house, you know, opening it up a bit, upgrading the kitchen and baths. I ran into Julian Martine at Starbucks and mentioned it to him, about the fact that you were getting married and would more than likely want to get things started as soon as possible. I asked him for a recommendation of an architect, maybe someone in his firm. With his reputation, it never occurred to me he'd have the time or inclination to take on a small job but you know Julian, anything for a friend. We met up at your place late this afternoon. Long story short, he went up into the attic to check the joists. You've had company, amigo, probably within the last couple of days. The footprints are fresh. It took us a couple of hours but we followed the wiring and got all the mics and transmitters. I've got Jace going in tomorrow to sweep my place too."

"Who did Forrest get to do the job, Maxwell Smart?"

"I can't deny it was sloppy and low-tech, but maybe he wanted you to find it, put you on notice that his dick was as big as yours."

"Or he didn't want any of the sophisticated stuff traced back to him."

"She's good for you, J.D. I wish I could make the rest of the bullshit go away, although I have to admit you're taking things a lot better than I thought you would."

"Oh, I'm pissed as hell, believe me. We need to beef up security anywhere there's a chance they'll try something again."

"Already being done. I've got three crews working all night and well into tomorrow. By the time you get your bride home, your place will be locked up tighter than Fort Knox."

"If I ever get her home."

"That sounds ominous." Sydney was walking toward us from the open bedroom door and my heart did that little jig it did every time I saw her. Wrapped from neck to toe in that god-awful bathrobe, her crazy copper hair pulled up and face scrubbed pink, she was the sexiest thing I'd ever seen.

"What's going on, boys?"

Her smile was radiant but there was something beneath it that made me want to grab my balls and run. I patted my lap and opened my arms. "Not much, honey, but I could sure use a hug." Like every other man who sensed he was in trouble, I believed if I sweet-talked her and threw in some lovin', I'd be okay. Then again, at one time I believed in Santa Claus too.

Passing right by me, she perched her butt on the arm of a chair and folded her arms. And then she brought forth the wrath of God. "Jordan, I love that you love me and want to protect me, I really do. God knows, I haven't had much of that in my life, but don't ever do that again, use gifts and sex as bribes. If the two of you need to discuss something of a confidential nature about IIF, just tell me and I'll leave the room. I don't have a problem with that. But if it's something that concerns me and I find out you're keeping it from me, for whatever reason, I'll make your life a living hell."

Dylan the ass-kisser tried to make nice. "Sydney, honey…"

Big mistake.

"Dylan, I love you like a brother. You've been a great mentor and a good friend, but the next time you chuck me under the chin like I'm three, be prepared to lose your hand. Now, if you'll both excuse me, I'm going to blow-dry my hair. You can call me when dinner gets here."

It takes a lot to make me speechless and I was pretty sure I'd never get it up again but she wasn't finished. When she reached the bedroom door, she turned back around and kicked us in the metaphorical nuts. "Being trained investigators and all, I suppose you've already considered the possibility that my father is trying to get rid of me for fear I'll throw a monkey wrench into his Senate campaign. And if that's the case, he's using Jeff. If I were him, I'd watch my back."

When she was out of earshot, I expected something wise and philosophical from Dylan, something about stress and anxiety or pre-wedding jitters, but he just grinned. "Is it me or was that hot?"

Ignoring for the moment that my woman made him hot, I had to agree. I'd wanted fireworks and I got them. And the best part? I got to keep my balls.

24

Forgiveness is one of the many horrible side effects of
loving someone.
—Randy K. Milholland

I had no illusions my ultimatum would work. In fact, I was pretty sure it accomplished diddly. They were who they were, big bad alpha males, and the world was safer with them in it.

Back in the bathroom, I was tempted to turn on the TV and catch up on the news, but the prospect of seeing myself, or worse my father, put an end to that. Our history said it all. He took immense satisfaction from encroaching on my happiness and I had to stop enabling him. These moments were mine.

Bent forward blow-drying my hair, I felt Jordan behind me, his thumbs hooked in the sash of the robe. I straightened up and our eyes met in the mirror.

"You're beautiful when you're angry."

You had to love a guy who looked you right in the eye and said the one thing that would piss you off. And despite his death wish, I did love him, loved him more than my life.

"My house was bugged. Dylan and a friend discovered it this afternoon."

He was trying his damndest to play it down but, again, I wasn't fooled. Like his passion, his anger was thinly-disguised, the tightening of his jaw, the way his chocolate eyes morphed to black.

I turned into him and laid my head against his chest. "So it's begun. He won't rest until he gets something on you, Jordan."

"He can't hurt us, sweetheart. You have to trust me."

If he truly believed that, we were in more trouble than I thought we were. "I do trust you, but he knows we're together, don't you see?"

"What I see is my woman upset and that's totally unacceptable."

You also have to love a guy who's the poster boy for chauvinism. As I saw it, I had three choices. I could go all psycho-feminista on his ass, or I could try to reason with him and point out the obvious, that dear old dad was mad as a hatter, or...

I chose door number 3. I'm only human after all, and he did look delicious standing there. I released the sash on the robe and let the whole thing pool at my feet. "Then perhaps you'd better do what you do best and take my mind off things."

If I thought he looked yummy before, my brash attempt to take *his* mind off things worked wonders. In one perfect moment, his lips twitched, his eyebrow shot up and his nostrils flared. "Is this make-up sex or a pity fuck?"

That struck me funny and I laughed. "Does it matter?" I was still laughing when he tossed me over his shoulder and made straight for the bedroom.

Dropping me on the bed, he took a half step back and snicked the buckle on his belt. "Hands and knees, little girl."

A breath away from issuing an order of my own, it occurred to me that we weren't alone, that Dylan was just outside in the living room. Clamping one hand over my mouth, I used the other to point to the door.

He flashed me a smile that held both threat and promise. "Make all the noise you want. Dylan went to his room to make some phone calls and check on room service."

He manipulated my body like an articulated doll. Within seconds, my knees were splayed near the foot of the bed, my head down facing the headboard. By the time he divested himself of his jeans, I was ready to combust, and judging from the way his cock stood high and proud, he was too.

Stepping up behind me, he ran his hands down my back and ass. When he got to my pussy, he slid an exploratory finger through my slit. "You have the most exquisite cunt I've ever seen, and I'm glad you're ready because this is going to be down and dirty."

A week ago, I might have cringed at the c-word, but a week ago I wasn't hot, horny and brazen as a banshee. "Yeah, yeah, yeah. If down and dirty is a euphemism for fast and hard, I'm your girl, cowboy."

His cock breached my channel in a single thrust, and true to his word, it was down and dirty, which made it no less hot. Then again, everything about the man was hot, not that I was biased.

When we eventually opened the door, Dylan was back. Grinning like a Cheshire cat, he did everything but pump the air.

Dinner was perfect. Back to being themselves, they regaled me with stories of their childhood that kept me laughing for hours. It was one of the best nights of my life. It felt so right, so comfortable, that I indulged in a glass of champagne.

Perhaps if I hadn't, things might have turned out differently. Or not. I knew from experience that bad days didn't come with warning labels and that the higher one flew, the worse the fall, that the more I reached for happiness, the harder the Fates worked to keep it from my grasp.

My mistake was believing in fairy tales.

25

"Daddy, don't, it hurts. Daddy!"

The words were bad enough but the little girl voice fucking killed me. Knowing not to wake her from the nightmare, I used the tips of my fingers to lift the hair from her face. "Shh, baby, I've got you. I'm right here."

But I wasn't there, not really. I was with *them*, the monster who raped her and the freak who let it happen, the same bastard who got off on knocking her around. My bloodlust at a peak, I held her in my arms and imagined a hundred scenarios for exacting revenge, for consigning their souls to that special Hell reserved for fiends.

When her breathing evened out and she was sleeping

peacefully, I slipped from the bed. There was just enough predawn light to see her face and I stood there for the longest time, staring at her, unable to remember what my life was like without her, before her beauty and her warmth, her humor and courage, her laughter and tears. As tempted as I was to wake her, to speak aloud what I was thinking, I didn't. She needed sleep and I needed some alone time.

I tried all my usual techniques, push-ups, sit-ups, even meditation, but like some diabolical loop inside my brain, that sad little voice refused to go away. By the time I stepped from the shower, the voice was quiet but the anxiety was back. I'd felt it earlier and tried to ignore it, the feeling that something was *off*, that I was missing something important. It was neither a good feeling nor a new one and I struggled with it. In fact, I fought it, fought it hard, right up to the second when my eyes fell on the thin strand of gold coiled around a locket, a locket with a hummingbird etched on the front.

Into my third cup of coffee, I was so engrossed in what I was reading that I didn't hear the bedroom door open. I glanced up as she veered away from me toward the room service tray. Dressed and ready for the day, she was wearing jeans and a tank top, her hair loose and wild the way I liked it.

I was a little put off she didn't speak up or bounce into my lap, but seeing me glaring into my laptop, she must have assumed I was working. She was considerate that way, low maintenance. It was something I noticed at the lake. Where some women would be angling for attention, she gave me room to work. I loved that about her, that streak of independence. And I hated it.

Maybe if she'd slept another hour, I would have had time to decompress, to see things through her eyes and put them in perspective. But I didn't. Righteously indignant, I saw only the lie.

"You had a nightmare, a bad one from the sound of it."

Even with her back to me, I read her body like a book. She tensed but her voice betrayed nothing. If anything, it sounded unnaturally perky. "Alcohol tends to bring them on. I guess I woke you up then, huh?"

"Yes, you did."

Turning, she looked at me as if I'd struck her. The look was fleeting, a millisecond, before she focused on the locket dangling from my fingers. She blanched and laid her hand against her throat. For long moments, she stared at the damn thing as if hypnotized. But now that I'd made my point, I wanted her attention on me. I closed my laptop with more force than was necessary and she jumped.

"Hummingbird. Not exactly a knee-slapper but the critics loved it. I assume you're familiar with it since you had a quote from it stuffed in your locket." I smoothed the crumpled paper I'd been holding in my hand and read it slowly, enunciating each word. *I hear him and I lock my soul in a shiny silver box. My heart beats and I will it to be still. He is the mist that hides the moon and haunts the sun.* I guess I don't have to tell you she's writing about her father. The rape started when she was five. You were, what, six the first time your father raped you?"

With a quick nod of her head, she wrapped her arms around herself. "You could have just asked me."

"I'm asking you now. You let me fuck you but you didn't trust me enough to tell the truth? Incest is…"

"Incest is what? Please don't presume to tell me what incest is, Jordan. I think I have a pretty good handle on it."

"Do you?" I rose from the sofa and started toward her but stopped when I saw her recoil. "Why the lie, Sydney?"

"I don't know why. I was ashamed and scared and I guess I thought it didn't matter."

"Everything matters."

"You're judging me, you with your perfect parents? Did they tuck you in at night? Did they stay with you while you said your prayers? Mine didn't. And what did you pray for, a new bike, good grades? I prayed for death. I prayed that God would take me to Heaven so my daddy wouldn't find me and crawl in bed with me."

"Jesus." That was the moment when I should have shut the fuck up or pled temporary insanity and thrown myself at her feet. But I didn't. "I'm not judging you, baby, but you need help. When things quiet down, we'll get you into therapy and deal with it."

Even a blind man could see I'd hit a nerve. Her eyes flashed and the resentment rolled off her in waves. "Why, because I didn't drop to my knees and bare my soul when you snapped your fingers? You can't control everything, Jordan. I'm not one of your submissives. I want your love, not your pity and certainly not your patronage."

In my attempt to find an outlet for my rage, I'd unleashed hers, and we stood there like two latter-day gladiators, swords and shields at the ready. Things were spiraling out of control, things I put in motion, and now I had to fix them before the rift became irreparable. I claimed the distance between us and cradled her face in my hands. "I'm not patronizing you and you have my love. You always will."

Laying her hands over mine, she whispered, "Will I?"

It took a moment for the words to sink in and even then I wasn't sure I'd heard right. I pulled back and studied her face. My ability to read a person's expression had saved my life more than once, but I was out of my element here, and I didn't like it one damn bit. In our short time together, I'd witnessed most of her moods, happy, sad, pensive, but this was new. Void of emotion, her eyes glassy and unfocused, this was a mask. One that screamed *retreat*.

A chill crept up my spine as I thought of the words in the locket, ones I'd lobbed at her in frustration. *I hear him and I lock my soul in a shiny silver box.* In my failure to distinguish lies from secrets, had I hurt her so badly that she was locking away a part of herself? Desperate to reconnect, I took her by the shoulders and shook her, not hard, but enough to draw her out from wherever she was hiding. "Sydney, for God's sake, look at me."

That brought her back, not all the way, but I was grateful for whatever I could get. As if pulling herself from a trance, she eventually gazed up at me. "I love you too. If you believe nothing else, please believe that."

I started to say something to reassure her when my cell phone signaled a text message. Since everyone but Dylan respected my disdain of texting, it wasn't hard to figure out the sender. In the second or two it took to get my priorities straight and ignore it, she'd turned away.

Were we done? I love you. You love me. That's it? In my experience with the fairer sex, it was never that simple. World peace was simple, fixing the deficit was simple; but a woman pissed was a woman on a crusade, and if the infidel was smart, he'd fall on his sword before things turned messy.

"I was wrong, sweetheart, and I'm sorry."

"You weren't wrong, Jordan. I may not like your interrogation techniques but I can't argue with your conclusions."

That was the scientist talking. It was the woman I wanted to hear from, the one who was even now rebuilding the defenses I'd spent the last four days dismantling. She was rubbing her temples, a device I'd used a time or two myself to avoid a discussion I didn't want to have. "Headache?"

"A little one. I think I'll take some aspirin and lie down."

Lie down? That's when it occurred to me she wasn't the only one in the room who needed therapy. While she was grappling with her emotions, I was struggling with a hard-on. In my mind, I saw her naked, her body spread before me on the bed. My fingers tingled with the feel of her, the silky smoothness of her skin. And her scent. God, I loved the way she smelled. Call it post-battle adrenalin, call it selfish, but I wanted her. And after she came screaming my name, she'd cuddle next to me while I told her all the things I was thinking earlier. Right before I lost my fucking mind.

"Jordan?" I came back down to earth to see her looking at me strangely, nodding at the cell phone clipped to my belt. "Your cell phone is chiming again."

Dylan was so dead, but the sooner I took care of his problem, the sooner I could get to mine. I'm not sure what I expected when I read the message but *Trouble* didn't make my top three choices.

It didn't take a genius to see she'd withdrawn back to Sydneyland, but at least she didn't ask about the text. If she had, I would have told her. Somehow, the idea of layering high-handedness with hypocrisy wasn't the best way to start off our wedding day.

After tearing Dylan's room number from the tablet on the desk, I went to her and wrapped her in my arms. "I'm stopping at Dylan's room before I go downstairs to run some errands. Stay in the room and don't answer the door unless you know who it is." I pulled back and planted a kiss on her forehead. "There's aspirin in my ditty bag. Try to get some sleep. I want my bride well-rested."

The smile she laid on me wasn't one of her best, but I took it as a sign I was forgiven. Right before I released her, she raised her hand to my cheek and whispered, "I'm sorry."

There was something familiar about the gesture, something I should have remembered but didn't. There were a lot of things I should have done before I left her, among them making sure she knew how much I loved her, but by then I was in action mode. I had to meet with Dylan, pull the bug from his ass and buy a wedding ring. And after what I put her through this morning, it was going to cost me a bundle.

Dylan looked like shit when he opened the door, from which I surmised that *Trouble* was an understatement.

"Fucking Forrest!"

Yep, we had trouble. Dylan could lose it with the best of them but the grunge look wasn't one he could pull off, nor was the lipstick smeared along his chin. It didn't take a trained investigator to figure out the evening hadn't ended when he left our room.

I shouldn't have grinned but I did. "Did you manage to fuck all the female performers from *Cirque du Soleil* or just the leads this time?"

He stepped aside and I stared into the familiar face of one of the biggest, baddest black dudes on the planet. "Sonofabitch."

172

"That's Special Agent Sonofabitch to you." Jerome Willis scowled before his face split into a smile and displayed a perfect set of brilliant white teeth. "How you doin', Captain?"

We did that thing guys do, a handshake followed by a quick hug and a manly slap on the back. "It's J.D. now. What the hell are you doing here?"

"You two know one another?" I couldn't tell if it was relief or disbelief on Dylan's face but I wished I'd brought my camera.

Willis hitched his thumb in my direction. "I was in Captain Dunham's unit. He saved my ass in Kosovo, pulled me from a burning jeep and carried me three miles. I guess I should have mentioned that part."

Running a hand through his hair, Dylan moved off to answer a knock at the door. "God, I hope that's coffee."

While he played host, Jerome and I played catch-up of the last ten-plus years, personal stuff about his wife and kids, buddies from our unit, that kind of thing. I didn't offer up information about my private life and Sydney wasn't mentioned. After an hour of small-talk, I was ready to cut to the chase. "I take it this isn't a social call. How long have you been with the Feds?"

"Ten years. I run the field office in New Haven, Connecticut. You've got some powerful friends and one nasty enemy, Captain."

"Forrest."

"He's making noise that you tried to murder his daughter and then kidnapped her when your plan ran amok. You know how these things go. The Bureau and the Agency have to make a show of playing nice."

"I assume he has something other than his big mouth to back up his claim."

"No, but we do. Two days ago, we got an anonymous call from a resident of Cambria. He claims he was walking his dog on Moonstone Beach when he heard the explosion. A couple of minutes later, he saw a late model black Escalade leaving the scene. He got a partial on the plate. Yesterday, a vehicle matching that description and registered to you was found at the San Luis Obispo airport and impounded. There were several drops of blood in the backseat that match Dr. Forrest's DNA on file with the Bureau. If you know where she is, I think it best you let me talk to her, Captain."

Anonymous my ass. The needle on my bullshit meter was deep in the red zone. Powerful friends or not, if the FBI suspected me of attempted murder, the room would be swarming with dark suits and Ray-Bans.

I'd forgotten Dylan was in the room until I heard him on his cell phone. Evidently he wasn't buying Willis's rationale either. When he was finished with the call, he sat back down. "At least part of his story is true. He does head up the field office in New Haven. Funny thing though, according to the Agent I spoke to, Special Agent Jerome Willis is on temporary leave."

In law enforcement parlance, *temporary leave* covered everything from forced downtime for psych problems to family issues, neither of which explained his presence. A more likely scenario was that he was on special assignment, one so uber-sensitive that he was operating alone and reporting to the top box on the organizational chart, FBI Director Herbert Miller. In the past, I might have enjoyed a game of cat and mouse but in the past I didn't have a warm and willing woman waiting in my bed. "I'm just spit-balling here, Jerome, but I think the reason you're in this room alone is because no one knows you're here but Miller, not even the locals. And since Greenwich is well within your jurisdiction, you're not here because of Sydney. You want Forrest."

Dylan snorted. "Take a number. Is this about Prentiss?"

Instead of the denial we were expecting, Jerome dropped his head and shook it. "Now I know why you guys get the big bucks. My mama would slap me upside the head for saying this but Prentiss got what he deserved. You dance with the Devil, you pay the price."

While I was enjoying the imagery, I wasn't giving him any information on Sydney until I knew where this was going. "What do you have on Forrest? And spare us the rhetoric about a continuing investigation."

"A month ago, a Bridgeport woman walked into our office with a story. She claimed that the previous month her young daughter was getting off the school bus a half block from their home when a blond man in a blue car grabbed her and drove her to another man who raped her. A few hours later, just after dusk, the little girl was dumped around the corner from the Emergency Room of Bridgeport Hospital. The hospital called the cops and did a rape kit on her. The examination evidenced severe vaginal tearing but no DNA. When she was calm enough for the cops to take her statement, she said the blond man who picked her up was wearing a baseball cap and sunglasses. She said he was younger than the man who did bad things to her. The cops had her look at mug shots but she was too traumatized to work with a sketch artist or provide them with anything helpful. A week or two after the rape, the mother and her daughter were having breakfast and the Sunday paper was on the table. The little girl started screaming and pointing at the paper. It was a photograph of Roger Forrest and his wife at some conservative fund-raiser. The mother knew what the cops' reaction would be so she came to us."

"I'm sure he's capable of it, but that's pretty thin," said Dylan. "How old is the little girl?"

"Six. And you're right. No prosecutor in his right mind would take on the Deputy Director of the CIA on the testimony of a six-year-old kid. But it got me thinking that maybe this wasn't the first time it happened, so I started looking into other unsolved cases involving the abduction and rape of little girls within a fifty mile radius of Greenwich. I got seven hits over a ten-year period, three in New Haven

County, two in Fairfield County and two in Westchester County, New York. I contacted the parents but none of them wanted to put their daughters through a second ordeal. I have three daughters so I had to respect their decisions. The most I could get out of the parents was the M.O. A blond man picked them up and took them to an older man who did the deed. The only inconsistency in their stories from the latest one was that the victims never saw the older man's face. They all said he did bad things to them in the dark."

Dylan got the look, the one that preceded his full-out shrink persona. "Forrest is a narcissist. He's been operating for ten years undetected and each rape has fueled his narcissism and belief that he's omnipotent. It's possible he knew the last rape was just that, the culmination of his spree, and he wanted to make it special. For him, the Senate is the Holy Grail, and he'll do whatever he has to do to make that happen, including giving up his hobby."

If this was a fishing expedition, I wanted off the boat. My empathy for the victims was exceeded only by my concern for Sydney. There was no way I'd let her be victimized again. The hoopla over her disappearance was hard enough on her, but if she had to relive her own molestation, the resulting media circus would make the current one seem like a cakewalk. The only thing the public liked better than a horrific murder was a sex scandal involving a prominent figure. Throw in a few salacious details about incest and rape, and like sharks in a feeding frenzy, the press would keep the water churned for months. With Sydney as the chum.

It was Dylan who asked the question I'd been avoiding. "Where does Sydney fit into all of this? From what I understand, she hasn't lived with her parents since she was sent off to prep school."

Reaching into the breast pocket of his jacket, Willis smiled. "I met her once at Quantico right after she started with the Bureau. She was sweet as could be. It was hard to believe she was Forrest's daughter."

As he was speaking, he was laying out photos of the victims, color photos, the kind you find in every parent's wallet. A quick glance confirmed they were all in the five to seven year range, all smiling and happy, and all with red hair.

Leaning in, Dylan mumbled something under his breath, glanced at Willis and then at me. I shot a look right back at him and hoped he got the hint.

Someone's cell phone was vibrating and I was relieved when it turned out to be Jerome's. I was even happier when he excused himself and stepped outside the room.

I waited a beat before nailing Dylan's ass to the wall. "You knew it was her father?"

"I suspected as much."

"And you didn't think a heads-up might be in order?"

"I gave you a heads-up by telling you to get her therapy. For all I knew, she concocted that story to keep from facing the truth about her father. It wouldn't be the first time. I had a fifty-year-old patient who swore up and down it was Mao Tse-tung who raped her when she was a kid. To some degree, we all lie to ourselves to make it through the day, but sooner or later we have to face the truth. The question now is what we tell Willis."

"We tell him nothing. If he wants Forrest, he can go after him for butchering his partner in crime, but I'm not putting her through an inquisition about the incest."

"Willis isn't stupid, J.D., and neither is Sydney. What if I'm wrong and the latest rape wasn't his last? What if Forrest molests another little girl and Sydney figures out she could have prevented it by coming forth about his pedophilia? And what happens when she discovers you took that decision away from her?" He got up to refill his coffee, a ploy to put some distance between his face and my fist. "I was in the room last night when she called both of us on our bullshit, remember? She isn't some urchin you picked up in your travels, amigo. She's a survivor and a respected scientist, a woman who went outside her comfort zone, danced naked in front of a hundred horny guys and nailed a serial killer from forty feet away. I've seen you two together and there's not a doubt in my mind this is the real thing. Don't blow it by trying to turn her into something she isn't."

"What the fuck is that supposed to mean?"

"You're a smart guy. You figure it out."

I didn't want to figure it out. What I wanted to do was go back upstairs, pack our things and get us as far away from this mess as possible. She was strong, I got that, but I was also in the room when I forced the truth about her father. I saw the child inside the woman, the anguish and pain. *You can't control everything, Jordan.* Maybe not. But I could sure as hell control this.

Willis chose that moment to re-enter the room. "I guess we're done here. Another victim just came forward and fingered Forrest as a pedophile. They've issued a warrant for his arrest."

For a guy who should have been doing handsprings, Willis looked uncomfortable, like he'd eaten one too many shrimp at the all-you-can-eat buffet. We said our quick good-byes and he was gone.

Dylan stood immobile, staring at the door. "Does it strike you as peculiar he didn't mention Sydney again?"

And I knew. I'm not sure how I knew, but I knew. Maybe it was the way Willis avoided eye contact when he came back from the phone call. Or maybe it was the gesture she made before I left our room, the one I should have remembered but didn't. It was right after we fired her. Convinced I couldn't have her and intent on having my say, I followed her to the lab. I said some lousy things to her that day but she just reached up, touched my cheek and said *I'm sorry.*

It was the last thing she did before she grabbed her things and ran.

26

It is easier to get forgiveness than permission.
—*Arthur Bloch, Murphy's Law Book Two*

Special Agent Richard Faber leaned back in his chair and steepled his fingers beneath his chin. "Let's see if I have this straight, Ms. Forrest. After being missing for four days, you waltz into our building, refuse to be debriefed about your disappearance and allude to the fact that the second most powerful man in U.S. Intelligence is responsible for not only the attempt on your life but the murder of Jeffrey Prentiss. Have I missed anything?"

Evidently looks couldn't kill so I did the next best thing and tried to match his arrogance with my own. "It's *Doctor* Forrest, Agent Faber, and you missed the part where I said I'd share the details of my rescue and information about my father only with Director Miller. You know the guy, big office, signs your paychecks."

"Director Miller is a busy man. That's why we have field offices and capable agents running them." Frowning, he ruffled the edge of a file with his thumb; a file he wanted me to believe had my name on it. "I'm familiar with your history with the Bureau, *Doctor*. Your former supervisor gave you high marks for competency but low marks for dealing with authority."

"My former supervisor thought his *authority* gave him free rein to grope me on a daily basis, but I don't see what relevance that has to the reason I'm here."

"It goes to your credibility, Doctor."

My bravado was shrinking almost as fast as my patience. Thirty-five minutes had elapsed since Jordan left the room and I went MIA. Knowing I had an hour, maybe two, before he discovered me gone, put two and two together and came busting through the door, I had to up the ante.

"Look, Agent Faber, I'll make this simple. You have ten minutes to put me in a room alone with a video feed to Director Miller or I'll walk out of here and take my story to *The New York Times*." I stopped short of threatening to include a word or two about the Bureau's insensitivity to sexual harassment issues but the look I threw at the file said it all.

It was hard to tell if he believed my bluff or not but at least it got him on his feet. "I'll see what I can do. Come with me."

Left in a room not much larger than a jail cell, I felt the stirrings of a panic attack. Monochromatic and sterile, the room was a study in grey, everything down to the table and chairs. There wasn't a hint of color anywhere, nothing to distract my mind, and within two or three minutes the solitude got to me. I even missed Agent Dick, his hostility a welcome diversion. With my emotional equilibrium already off-kilter, the last thing I wanted to do was revisit the events which led me there or those final hurtful moments in the suite. My traitorous psyche disagreed.

For the umpteenth time that morning, a verse from John Lennon's *Beautiful Boy* popped into my head. *Life is what happens to you while you're busy making other plans.* In the past, I'd thought that quote brilliantly insightful. Now I just found it annoying.

Over dinner, Jordan had mentioned his intention to get up early and check out the hotel's fitness facilities, so I thought nothing of it when I woke up alone. Blissfully unaware of the nightmare, I stretched like a contented cat. If yesterday's down and dirty encounter was a jam session, the one that followed Dylan's late-night departure was a symphony. Jordan's virtuoso performance left every cell in my body tingling in remembrance. I felt cherished and adored, sublimely happy.

Lying there wrapped in his scent, I reached for the TV remote with the belief that the world outside our suite did not exist. I believed that love conquered all and we were invincible. I was even foolish enough to believe that my father's misdeeds, however despicable, could never touch me again, that his hold on me was severed. How delusional was I?

. . . the decapitated remains discovered yesterday in a suburban neighborhood of El Paso, Texas, have been identified as those of Jeffrey Stanhope Prentiss III of Greenwich, Connecticut. Wanted for questioning by the FBI in the attempted murder and subsequent disappearance of Sydney Forrest...

I made it to the bathroom just in time. After throwing up the remnants of last night's supper, I stretched out on the cool marble floor and gave in to the tears, tears for Jeff, for his parents, for myself. What propelled me into action was imagining Jordan, his body bruised and battered, another victim of my father's madness.

I had no choice. I knew what I had to do but *how* to do it was a problem. Since I wasn't sure when Jordan left for the gym, I couldn't predict when he'd be back. Finding me skulking through the hotel would result in a lengthy war of wills, one I'd never win. My best bet was to wait for his return and send him on an errand. When he left the room, I'd slip out and do my thing. He'd be pissed to find me gone but I'd take angry over dead any day.

As I showered and dressed, I settled on a plan. Attempting to make my case to the Las Vegas P.D. would be a waste of time. If they didn't mire me in questions, they'd bury me in red tape. My best hope was the Bureau, a model of efficiency. I could tell my story, sign a statement and be back in time to face the music. Assuming everything went off without a glitch, we could still make the chapel by four.

Opening the bedroom door and finding Jordan hunched over his laptop threw me for a loop. The atmosphere felt charged, heavy and oppressive like right before a storm. The girlie part of me wanted to shove the computer aside and find shelter in his lap, but my practical side knew something was amiss. Respecting his need to work through whatever crisis was afoot, I made a silent beeline for the coffee tray.

The wait was short, the ensuing confrontation not my finest hour. It was one thing to be caught in a lie, another to be caught by someone who equated prevarication with betrayal. Defensible or not, it was a lie born out of shame not malice, and it enraged me that he didn't know the difference. He didn't know me.

Things went sideways after that, but the real conflict was taking place inside my head. Intellectually, I knew Jordan's wrath was directed at my father, but my emotional self felt the sting of his words nonetheless. *You need help.* The subtext was as clear as if he'd screamed it. *I want a healthy woman, Sydney, and you don't fit the bill.*

Most of which followed was a blur. I sensed Jordan speaking to me, touching me, but the only voice I heard was my father's, his recent litany of *Bitch, Cunt, Whore* replaced with an indictment he'd hurled at me more times than I could count. *Failure.*

Nothing says *happily ever after* like a wedding day dust-up, but at least I saw my previous anxiety for what it was, fear that I would fail at love, that in the cold light of day I wouldn't measure up. Perhaps Jordan sensed it too and his subconscious was looking for an out. He wasn't the type of man who would renege on a commitment, and even if he were willing to share our bed with a murderer and rapist, I wasn't.

The easy part would be blowing the whistle on my father. Purging him from my soul would take time. Jordan was right. I needed help, professional help, and as much as I loved him, it was a journey I had to make alone.

The Las Vegas office of the FBI is 7.45 miles from the Bellagio, twelve minutes by taxi. That's seven hundred and twenty seconds, one for each of my regrets. The one that stood out, the one that swamped me in remorse was that I didn't leave a note. At the very least, I should have absolved him of guilt. I thought about it, really I did. In those first few minutes when he left the room and I was gathering my things, I thought of nothing else. There was simply too much to say and too little time. And anyway, what was the point? Shouldering blame was an occupational hazard for superheroes. I was counting on the fact that their job description also included forgiveness.

"Dr. Forrest? Sydney?" I swallowed the lump in my throat and looked up into the face of Agent Faber. He wasn't smiling, but he wasn't glaring at me either. "I owe you an apology. I just got off the phone with Director Miller and apparently there are things in play here I wasn't aware of."

That made two of us. What *things*? "Has he agreed to talk to me?"

Signaling a lull in the conversation, he raised a finger as two new people entered the room. A woman left a carafe of coffee and bottle of water on the table and a youngish man ran power to a laptop and booted it up. When the door closed behind them and we were alone, Faber nodded at the laptop. "You're all set. The Director will be with you in a minute. Even guys with big offices who sign paychecks have to answer Nature's call from time to time."

Agent Dick had a sense of humor. Who knew? I got to my feet and extended my hand. "I'm sorry too. It's been a rough morning and I've been told I can be a handful."

He shook my hand and smiled. "I've got one home just like you and I wouldn't have it any other way. Unfortunately, being a hardass comes with the territory. I'll be in my office if you need me."

Now that it was happening, I was shaking in my espadrilles. Everything hinged on Miller believing me. What if he didn't? There were no witnesses, no corroborating evidence, nothing to back up my story. Besides Amanda, Mike and Jordan, no one knew about the sexual abuse. Looking back, I was sure there were those who suspected, a teacher, my pediatrician, but the indomitable Roger Forrest was a master at deception. When I turned twenty-one, I tried to get a copy of the report filed by Connecticut Child Protective Services and found it missing along with any notation of the visit. There was a good chance I was screwed. If I couldn't get Miller to at least hear me out, Jordan was a dead man. And if that happened...

"You gave us quite a scare, young lady."

Director Miller's presence filled the screen and I tried to recall everything I'd heard about him, anything that would help me make my case. Texas born and bred, he was a colorful character. Known for being intelligent and fair, he was a man of few words, a straight-shooter who expected those around him to get to the point and move on. I could do that.

"Director Miller, I want to thank you for..."

Identical to the gesture Faber used, Miller raised a single digit and stopped me mid-sentence. "Is there a reason Agent Willis didn't accompany you from the hotel?"

The question startled me, but I had the good sense to keep my cool. "I don't know an Agent Willis, Sir. I came here alone in a taxi."

He raised an eyebrow, the universal man-tic for intimidation, but it didn't even faze me. Compared to Jordan, Miller was an amateur. He'd also shown his hand. If the FBI knew we were in Vegas then they also knew Jordan and Dylan were involved in my disappearance. And if that were the case, they could be prosecuted for hindering an investigation. Over my dead body.

"Director Miller, I came here about my father but before I get to that, I want your assurance that neither Jordan Dunham nor Dylan Hunt are at risk for prosecution. Jordan saved my life and Dr. Hunt took care of my injuries after the explosion. They took me somewhere to heal, somewhere to…" My voice broke and I struggled to maintain my composure.

"Sydney, you have my word we're not interested in them. You told Agent Faber you believed your father was involved in the attempt on your life and the murder of Jeffrey Prentiss. Roger Forrest is an important man with political aspirations which extend all the way to the White House. Obviously I need more than your say-so. I need a motive."

"He raped me. From the age of six until I reached puberty, he raped me every chance he got and when he couldn't do that anymore, he…oh, God."

I lost it. Right there in that horrid little room, I completely unraveled. It wasn't the pain of dredging up the trauma from my childhood. It was the knowledge that nothing I said would make a difference. Connecticut's statute of limitations on rape and sexual assault had long since run out, and it was my word against his, a respected public figure.

When I pulled myself together, I redirected my attention to the screen. "It's not enough, is it? He's going to get away with all of it, Jeff's murder, the rape…"

"My dear girl, thanks to you and for reasons I can't divulge at this time, he's not going to get away with any of it. Do you need a moment?"

I instinctively knew not to press him for an explanation. It was sufficient that I trusted him. And I didn't need a bloody moment. I needed Jordan, but since I couldn't have him, I wanted to finish up and get out of that room before I lost it again. "I'm fine, sir. What else do you want to know?"

"I have enough to ensure that your father is in for a very bad evening. Why don't I have Agent Faber take you back to your hotel and tomorrow morning we can pick up where we left off."

I could have lied, perhaps I should have, but trust is a two-way street. Every word I'd spoken was the truth and it felt wrong to change the rules halfway through the game. "I'm not going back to the hotel. Jordan and Dylan have done enough. Once the press gets wind of the incest, they'll rummage through every aspect of my life and I don't want them embroiled in this mess."

Maybe I fudged the truth a little but I had neither the energy nor the inclination to share the gory details of my love life. And it wasn't a lie. IIF could only be effective if it operated in anonymity. The publicity could ruin them.

"I see. Where can I contact you?"

I should have anticipated that question but the fact was I had no idea where I was going. Other than my passport and the hundred dollar bill Jordan had slipped into my pocket during the drive from Tahoe, I had nothing but my watch. It was a Rolex, a gift from my grandfather when I graduated High School. If I pawned it, it might bring a few hundred dollars, enough for a bus ticket somewhere and a cheap hotel room. Airport security being what it was, I couldn't risk a commercial flight nor could I risk going home. It was the first place everyone would look.

"I'm not sure where I'll be. Can I get back to you?"

"Sydney, it was one thing when you were under the protection of Dunham and Hunt, but in all good conscience I can't leave you in the wind. As of five minutes ago, you're a material witness in a criminal investigation and, as such, I have no choice but to take you into protective custody." He saw the expression on my face and must have known exactly what I thought of that idea because he raised that damn finger again. "And before you get your knickers in a knot, let me explain. We'll get you on a plane within the hour, fly you here and ensconce you in a safe location. Tomorrow, when you're rested, we'll finish taking your statement about the sexual assault and your father's relationship with Jeffrey Prentiss. How does that sound?"

It sounded like another alpha male trying to push me around, but knowing it wasn't a request, I folded my arms across my chest and put as much rancor in my response as I dared. "If you insist, Sir, but I draw the line at Witness Protection as a long-term solution."

"There are alternatives, Sydney. With your credentials and the Bureau's connections, I'm sure we can find you a position somewhere that will suit your needs."

A *temporary* position, just until I got my head on straight and the press found someone else to hound, a month, two at the most. Anything beyond that was inconceivable.

27

"Rise and shine, amigo. We need to talk."

I heard the rattle of the blinds a second or two before the sunlight stabbed my eyelids. If I'd been in any shape to find my gun, I'd have shot the bastard.

Dylan swept a pile of clothes and an empty liquor bottle from the only chair in the room and settled in. "They got the guy who did the hit on Prentiss. He washed out of the Agency in '08, but he and Forrest kept in touch. The Feds picked him up in a bar in Alabama and he sang like a little girl. They're throwing the book at Forrest. He'll be lucky if he doesn't get a needle in his arm. Maybe now that she knows her old man's going away for good..."

"Save it." I threw back the sheet, swung my feet to the floor and scrubbed my hands over my face. The beard was new but the pain in my gut was old news.

"It's only been three months, J.D."

Only three months? That was like a doctor walking in the room and announcing you *only* had cancer. Three months was an eternity when the thing I wanted most was excised from my life. Knowing it was my hand that held the scalpel only made the pain worse. "What the hell day is it anyway?" My eyes hadn't quite adjusted to the light but I could tell from his exasperated sigh that the question ticked him off.

"It's Sunday. Look, I know we agreed you could take all the time you needed to find her but..."

"I'm not pulling my weight." I figured that was coming. Aside from a day here and there, I'd pretty much relinquished the running of IIF to Dylan. Cases were already piling up when I was in Bahrain, so I wasn't sure how he was managing while I was off chasing ghosts.

"I'm thinking of bringing Jared and Ian back on-board for a few months, J.D. It's either that or close the doors."

That woke me up. "Is this your way of asking for my resignation?"

"Is this your way of asking for my boot up your ass? We've been partners since we were ten, but if you want out, just say the word. But before you shoot your mouth off again and spend the *next* three months feeling sorry for yourself, consider this. Is that what Sydney wants? I know you've been beating yourself up all this time thinking you ran her off with your macho crap but what if you're wrong? When the news broke about the incest and Forrest was arrested for rape, not one reporter came nosing around IIF. You think that would have been the case if the two of you were together? What if she's staying low to keep the press from breathing down our necks?"

It wasn't much of a lifeline but I grabbed it like a drowning man. "You really believe that?"

"I believe she's crazy in love with you and she's proving it by keeping her distance. When this mess with her father dies down, she'll come back, mark my word." He looked around the room and shook his head. "I keep remembering that last night in Vegas, how we laughed when she said you had the soul of a superhero. If she walked in here right now, I wonder what she'd think."

"If that's your idea of tough-love, you suck at it." The fact that there was more than a grain of truth in what he said didn't score any points either. "You going somewhere? That's the second time you've looked at your watch in the last five minutes."

"Yeah, I'm going somewhere, and if you ever bothered to read your emails or listen to your voicemails, you'd know I'm flying to Seattle to speak at the APA Conference. I'll be back Wednesday night. Jared's flying in tonight to cover the office. Grace emailed him a status report with all current and pending cases."

"Is that what you want?"

"What I want? Thanks for asking, asshole. What I want is my best friend back with his woman at his side. I want to stop here on a Sunday morning and mooch brunch and watch the two of you acting like a couple of lovesick teenagers. But since that's not going to happen until she's ready, I'll settle for having my partner back."

I'm a yeller, but for a guy who rarely raised his voice, Dylan was giving me a run for my money. It was also the kick in the ass I needed. "Give me the goddamn report."

"I emailed it to you an hour ago. Welcome back, superhero." Halfway out the door, he turned around and jerked his head toward the empty liquor bottle. "Stay away from the kryptonite."

I waited till I heard the front door slam and shuffled to the bathroom. A quick look in the mirror confirmed the worst. Alcohol, fast food and one too many sleepless nights had taken their toll, and as much as it annoyed me to admit it, Dylan had a point. If Sydney walked back into my life right now, she might just turn up that perfect little nose and walk back out. Mentally and physically, I had to get back in the game.

In the past three months, I'd logged more air miles than a flight attendant. Determined to find her and bring her home, I followed every lead. All anyone had to do was hint at a sighting and I'd grab my bag and go. My first trip East, I ambushed Willis and used the I-saved-your-butt card, but that was a waste of time too. If he knew where she was, he wasn't talking. About the only thing he'd say was she was safe, to which I took exception. She wouldn't be *safe* until she was tucked into the crook of my arm or snuggled beside me in bed. But before she got tucked and snuggled, I was going to beat her sweet ass for this latest hare-brained stunt. Lacing up my running shoes, I smiled for the first time in months.

I wasn't sure if it was Dylan's wake-up call or the endorphin rush from the run, but by the time I got back, I felt looser, less strung out. Hot and sweaty, I stepped into the shower and jacked off to an image of Sydney's little body draped across my lap, those curvy butt cheeks red from my hand. She was in so much fucking trouble.

After grabbing some coffee, I settled into my home office, turned on my laptop and printed out the report. Had I been smart, I would have concentrated on the task at hand but, being me, I did the dumbest thing I could do. I slipped in the disc from *Naughty Nellie's*.

With the sound off and nothing to distract me, I drank in every movement, each and every sexy sway. The depression hit me like a freight train. When the walls closed in and my chest tightened up, I stumbled through the open French Doors and out to the deck. Bracing my arms against the railing, I lowered my head and tried to get some air back in my lungs. "Just let me know I haven't fucked it up, baby. That's all I ask."

I didn't recognize the sound at first. Outside of the airport gift shop where I'd picked it off a display, I'd never heard it make so much as a tinkle. It was during one of my first trips after Vegas when I still believed that finding her would be a piece of cake. I'm not sure what possessed me to buy it, other than the little dangly things were in the shape of a hummingbird. I thought she'd get a kick out of it, so I brought it home and hung it outside the kitchen window where it could catch the wind. And then I forgot about it. Until now. The damn thing was going crazy, or I was. It was chiming up a storm but the air around it was dead still, not even the hint of a breeze.

"You asked me why I wasn't in the car when it exploded, why I stopped and turned around. I heard wind chimes. . .

A skeptic by nature, I'd learned there were things in life you had to take on faith. There was no earthly explanation for it, but a dead woman had saved Sydney's life, I was sure of it. If Theresa was trying to tell me to hang in there and not give up, the least I could do was pay attention.

Nine months later, I'd almost convinced myself the incident with the wind chime never happened. I chalked it up to stress, booze and anything else I could think of. A few times I'd even yanked it off the hook and tossed it in the trash, but I always plucked it out before it wound up in a landfill.

IIF was purring along. It took a few months, but we were

finally back on track. With the world more fucked up than ever, we'd had to hire some people to cover the hot spots, but other than a week here or there to put out a fire, I stayed close to home.

Physically, I was in the best shape of my life. During the remodeling of my house, Julian had managed to eke out enough square footage for a modest home gym. Working out helped take the edge off so I could sleep.

He'd done wonders with the house. A few years ago when the California real estate market began to tank, I bought it for a song so I was able to sink some money in it where it would do the most good. It was the second smartest thing I'd done in awhile. The first was giving Julian carte blanche to do whatever he thought best. The results were amazing. He'd turned a ho-hum house into a showplace. It needed only one thing to make it a home, the one thing my money couldn't buy. Sydney.

Coming up on a year, I knew that ship had sailed and with it my plans for our future. She'd always be the love of my life, my first thought in the morning and my last at night, but the time had come to face the final stage of grief, acceptance.

What would have been our one-year anniversary was a few days away and I intended to spend it in Tahoe watching action movies and getting shit-faced. With my duffel bag already stowed in the SUV, the plan was to sneak out early and get a jump on Friday traffic.

Logging off my computer, I looked up to see Dylan

standing in the doorway of my office. "We have a situation. I just got off the phone with…"

I did my best to ignore him. Unless the *situation* involved Steven Segal and a bottle of fifty-year-old Scotch, I didn't want to hear about it.

"…Jacques Villier. He wants a meeting in his office Tuesday morning."

My ears pricked up. It wasn't every day that France's Minister of Defense wanted a sit-down. "What the hell for?"

"He was reluctant to get into specifics on the phone but I gather it has something to do with the upcoming G8 Summit. You've got an hour to go home and pack. We'll take the jet to Phoenix. Grace got us on a red-eye to New York and we'll fly from there to Paris tomorrow night. We'll have Sunday and Monday to rest up."

"You might be flying to Paris tomorrow night but I have other plans."

"He wants both of us, J.D. What other plans?"

I could hear the wheels turning in his head and I didn't have time for twenty questions. "I'm going to Tahoe."

He narrowed those baby blues at me. "The hell you are. You're not going off alone to lick your wounds and stick me with Villier. It's Paris, amigo, the City of Light, good food, fine wine and…"

"Forget it. I hate Paris, I hate French food and their wine gives me a headache."

28

"Steak au Poivre medium rare, pommes frites and a bottle of the Bourgogne Rouge 2007. Merci." Returning the menu to the waiter, I shot a scowl across the table at Dylan. At the very least I expected a grin, at worst some wiseass comment. Happily for him, I got neither.

He knew damn well I didn't hate Paris. I loved the city, so much in fact that it was where I'd planned to take Sydney for our honeymoon. It was the memories I detested, the ones that skittered through my brain and landed in my stomach with a thud.

"Let it go, amigo. Play your cards right and you might even get lucky tonight."

It was clear his plans for the evening were more ambitious than mine. I'd be lucky just to get through dinner, manage a brisk walk back to the hotel and fall asleep without benefit of pharmaceuticals. I travelled enough to know that the only thing separating me from a blithering idiot was sufficient shut-eye. Unfortunately, between time changes, layovers and enough caffeine to reanimate a corpse, I was wired to the max.

"Dylan...Jordan?"

We were waiting for espressos when a breathy voice floated over my shoulder. One look at Dylan's face as he rose from the banquette told me I wasn't hallucinating.

Getting to my feet, I stood there like some mindless twit and let Dylan handle the pleasantries. "Sydney, my God, what a surprise. What are you doing here? You look fantastic."

Fantastic didn't cut it. I'm not sure a word has been invented to describe the way she looked. I wasn't prepared to see her at all but to see her like this left me speechless. Dressed for a night on the town, she was wearing some basic black number that hugged her curves and stopped an inch or so above her knees. My gaze strayed to the strappy black stilettos before returning to her face. It was Sydney's face but different, darker lashes, redder lips. Sexy and sultry, she took my breath away.

"I live here." Responding to Dylan but looking at me, the need in her eyes was so desperate that I almost caved. Almost. When it was obvious I wasn't going to acknowledge her or make a move toward her, she lowered her lashes.

She appeared guilty as hell and I assumed it had something to do with the guy hovering beside her, the GQ model with the George Clooney hair and Gerard Butler scruffy face, the one I wanted to take outside and pound into the pavement.

Her voice was shaky as she made the introductions. "Philippe Dumont, this is Jordan Dunham and Dylan Hunt. Philippe and I work together."

Been there, done that. One day you were the picture of professional propriety and the next day you were sucking her clit. And then she'd leave you high and dry without a note.

Philippe stepped forward and extended his hand. "Gentlemen, a pleasure. Sydney speaks of you often."

Did she now.

Sensing things were about to turn ugly, Dylan tried to avert it by sucker-punching me. "We've just finished dinner but you're welcome to join us for coffee."

Second only to a colonoscopy, I could think of few things more fun than chatting up my former fiancée and her current fuck buddy, a sentiment I was preparing to share with the entire café when Philippe shook his head.

"Actually, we were just leaving when Sydney spotted you. We had an early supper so we could make the opera." He smiled down at her. "Cherie, if you would prefer to spend the evening with your friends, I can assure you I will not be offended in the least." He snapped his fingers and turned to

Dylan. "Unless, of course, you would like to join me, Dr. Hunt. Sydney mentioned your fondness for opera."

Dylan had a fondness for opera like I had a fondness for genital herpes, but I was curious where this was going.

Her face lit up as she looked from one man to the other. "Would you mind? I'd love to speak with Jordan alone."

I hadn't seen her smile in a year and I reveled in it. It was too bad I had to destroy it. "Some other time."

Her head whipped around and I thought I saw her eyes fill, which might have been a trick of the light. "Please, Jordan, just a few minutes."

I was like a junkie reunited with his fix. As impossible as it seemed, I wanted her more than ever, but I knew a few minutes wouldn't satisfy my craving. Besides, I wasn't in to sloppy seconds. "This has been fun. We should do it again next year."

As an exit line it could have been better but I think she got the gist. Ignoring the disapproving looks of Dylan and Philippe, I threw a wad of Euros on the table and beat a retreat for the exit.

The cool night air helped clear my head, and by the time I reached the hotel I had a few things figured out. A half hour later, I'd paced a trail in the carpet and was contemplating which wall to put my fist through when Dylan knocked at my door.

As tempting as it was to put *him* through the wall, which

sounded even better than my fist, I popped a cap on a beer from the mini-bar and handed it to him. "We've had each other's backs for thirty years. You want to tell me why you let her set me up?"

"She didn't set you up, J.D. She didn't know anything about it. Philippe and I set you up."

I'll admit that knocked the shit out of me. In a single night, I'd lost my woman and my best friend. "If you had to prove to me she's moved on, you might have found a better way than conspiring with her lover."

"Christ, you're an ass. He's not her lover, he's her psychiatrist. Now you can kick my butt all over this hotel room or you can sit down and hear me out and maybe even salvage what's left of your relationship with her. Which is it?"

If those were my only choices, it was a no-brainer. "Start talking."

"I met Philippe nine months ago at the American Psychiatric Association conference in Seattle. The last day the topic was Ethics and how the lines are being blurred in the interest of national security and law enforcement. It was interesting enough but nothing I didn't already know. A couple hours later, a few of us were in the bar downstairs and the subject came up about attachments between psychiatrists and their patients, a subject as old as psychiatry itself. More often than not, it's the patient who forms an attachment to the doctor, but after awhile the discussion took a decidedly different turn and we started discussing women, or men as the case may be, who we didn't so much want to treat as fuck. The more we drank, the more we spilled our guts, everyone except this one guy who got up from the bar and took a seat at a table all by himself. It was Philippe. He was one of the speakers earlier in the day. He has a practice here in Paris but he also consults for the Sûreté. I was bored, so I grabbed my drink and joined him. After a few minutes, he looked over at the group at the bar and started talking about a woman he'd been treating for the past month, a colleague. He met her when she joined the Forensic Science Institute in Paris. He never mentioned her name. All he'd say was she was American, brilliant, and one of the most beautiful women he'd ever seen. He said he almost refused to take her on as a patient because he was afraid he'd fall in love with her, but she begged him. She told him she was desperately in love with a man back in the States but her father would always come between them unless she got help. He specializes in incest and child abuse cases, J.D."

I'd had the wind taken out of my sails a few times before in my life, but nothing like this. "One year, Dylan. You watched me go out of my mind for a fucking year and you've known all along where she was?"

"Technically I've only known for nine months. And what would you have done if I'd told you where she was? I'll tell you exactly what you would have done because I would have done the same thing and I know better. You would have taken the next plane to Paris and dragged her ass back. And a week later or the month after that, the same problem would have reared its ugly head. I dealt with rape and incest every day in my practice but that's not the same as living it. Her bastard father raped and physically abused her and she's lived with that betrayal and horror all her life. You wanted to fix her, J.D., but she was smart enough, even if you weren't, to know she had to fix herself."

"Nine months is a long time. For all you know, they're a couple now."

He gaped at me as if I'd grown a second head. "Have you always been this obtuse? I don't know what the woman sees in you. They're not a couple, they're friends. Before I left him that night in Seattle, I told him I knew who she was and to let me know when he released her from treatment. He called me last week. That's why we're here. I'll admit the reunion could have gone better. What the hell were you thinking?"

"I wasn't thinking. I was reacting. I saw her with Philippe and thought I'd lost her. I'll never forget the way she looked at me when I stomped out of there. It was the same look that was on her face the day we fired her and I let her have it in the lab, the same look as that morning in Vegas when I confronted her about her father. What kind of monster does that make me, a man who not once, not twice but three times hurts the thing he loves most in the world?"

"It makes you a monster of the flaming asshole variety, and if it'll make you feel better, it would be my pleasure to kick *you* around this hotel room." He pulled a slip of paper from his pocket and held it out to me. "Or maybe your time would be better spent going after your woman. What do you think?"

I snatched the paper from his fingers. "I think I owe you one."

"You owe me more than one, amigo. And that comment about you getting lucky tonight? I'm revising it. You'll need more than luck. You'll need a miracle."

29

'Tis the most tender part of love, each other to forgive.
—John Sheffield

Amanda was forever teasing me about being schizophrenic, while I preferred to think of myself as a paradox. Case in point: I accepted evolution as scientific fact but I also embraced the belief in a higher power. In my opinion, those who found the theories mutually-exclusive and railed against either position were just wrong-headed. Similarly, I saw no conflict with being a realist *and* an incurable romantic, although I am rethinking that one.

I never took a poll or anything, but I was sure I wasn't the first woman to want a movie moment with the man she loved. For twelve long months, I imagined our eventual encounter like the final minutes of *An Affair to Remember.* Channeling

Cary Grant, Jordan would bluster, forgive me and profess undying love. What I got was the shower scene from *Psycho*.

Philippe didn't know whether to comfort me or follow Jordan from the restaurant and beat him to a pulp. Ditto Dylan. I had two brilliant shrinks at my disposal and neither of them knew what to do with me. When we took the party outside, I threw my hands up in disgust and hailed a cab. As it pulled away, I glanced back through the rear window and saw them arguing, oblivious to the fact that I'd left. Did every man on the planet suck?

Safely back in my apartment, I put the kettle on for tea and retreated to the bedroom to change clothes. For my first night out in months, I'd wanted to feel like a woman again. I was going for sophisticated when I bought the dress and shoes and went a bit exotic on the make-up. Several hours after the fact, my full-length mirror told a different story. Hootchie-Mama Barbie maybe, Audrey Hepburn not so much. I really needed to get past the whole Hollywood thing.

I sent the shoes flying one way, the dress another, and changed into warm-ups and a t-shirt. Tea in hand, I circumnavigated the half-packed cartons in the living room and curled into one end of the sofa, my comfort spot. The boxes mocked me. I hadn't told anyone, not even Philippe, but in three weeks I was going home, or what I hoped would be my home. With the help of a realtor I'd found on-line, I signed a six-month lease on a small house in Paso Robles, a stone's throw from IIF. The plan was to settle in, contact Jordan and…and now what?

I gave in to a fresh surge of tears and did what I always do when the sadness creeps in. I took inventory of my life. Present evening notwithstanding, the past year had left me with more good things than bad. I'd made new friends, re-established contact with some old ones and received one amazing gift.

The therapy was much more intense than I thought it would be, but I didn't regret a single moment. When my father copped a plea and accepted life without parole, the tears I shed were for his victims, eight little girls whose only sin was looking like me. The day after his sentencing, the BBC reported that my mother was filing for divorce and checking herself in to Betty Ford. Wanting to show my support and hoping for some kind of relationship, I wrote her several letters but never heard back. I wished her well.

The only other apartment on my floor was owned by a charming Russian writer who was old enough to be my grandfather. For some reason, he got it in his head that my name was *Melbourne,* and I never had the heart to correct him. One or two evenings a week, he'd drop by, read me what he'd written and we'd share a cup of tea. I hadn't seen him in a few days so when the knock came on my door, I was grateful for the company.

"Goddamn it, Sydney. Didn't anyone ever teach you not to open the door to strangers?" Jordan gave me the once-over.

"Now I know what happened to my *Sloppy Joe's* t-shirt. It was my favorite, by the way."

My mouth dropped open. I was trying to decide which of his asinine comments to address first when he picked me up around the waist, set me out of his way and walked past me like he owned the place. "I thought you were at the opera."

I closed the door and pressed back against it to keep from falling over. "Then why are you here? If you were planning to break in and steal the silver, be my guest. It will be one less thing to box up."

Ignoring my sarcasm, he started poking around in some of the boxes. "Where are you running to this time?"

If you hadn't gone all Norman Bates on me, I'd be running back to you, you big jerk. That's what I would have said if I'd had my wits about me, but I was too busy reminding myself that jumping his bones would be counterintuitive. Aside from looking even more amazingly ripped, he hadn't changed a bit. He was still the most gorgeous man on this or any other continent. "What do you want, Jordan?"

He didn't answer me at first, just stared at me, those dark eyes setting me on fire. "I want a lot of things, Sydney, but what I want right now are some answers. I want to know what was going through your head the day you walked out on me. I want to know how you could let me twist in the wind for a year without a single goddamn word from you."

So this was nothing more than a fact-finding trip after all.

Well, fine. I'd give him what he wanted. He deserved that much. "There's a box on the bottom shelf of the end table by the sofa. Everything you want to know is in there. Just take it and leave."

He retrieved the box and began sifting through it. "There must be a couple hundred sealed envelopes in here and they're all addressed to me."

"Actually, there are three hundred and sixty-four letters or emails, one for each day since I left Las Vegas. I wrote you every night. If you'd come an hour later, there would have been another one." *The last one.*

He put the box aside and started toward me. Cupping my face in his hands, he swiped at my tears with his thumbs. "Give me the highlights. Better yet, tell me how you signed off on the one you wrote last night."

I closed my eyes and let the warmth of his caress repair my broken heart. "I signed off by saying that every moment away from you was torture and I loved you with all my heart."

"That's my girl." He brushed my lips with his. It wasn't the most passionate kiss we'd ever shared but it was definitely the sweetest. "I lied when I said there were a lot of things I wanted. All I want is you."

"Explain that."

He gave me that slow, sexy grin, the one that always made my panties wet. "You want the scientific version, the stuff about pheromones and testosterone?"

"Will it put me to sleep?"

"It will if I do it right." He wiggled his eyebrows. "And I always do it right."

It felt as if every erogenous zone in my body was suddenly awakening from a coma. I needed him inside me more than I needed my next breath. "And when we get out of bed?"

"Who said we were getting out of bed? You know, the last thing Dylan said to me before I left the hotel was that I'd need a miracle. I guess he was wrong."

A miracle, huh? My knees went weak and my heart rate kicked into overdrive. It was now or never.

Sensing my trepidation, Jordan took me by the shoulders and held me at arms' length. "What's wrong?"

"Nothing's wrong. In fact, something's incredibly right but…"

"But what, baby?"

"Do you still want me like before, like forever?"

"Forever isn't nearly long enough, but if you're asking if I still want to marry you, I've never wanted anything more in my life." That damn grin was back. "It's probably the only way I'll get my t-shirt back, and I really like that t-shirt. I got it in Key West when Dylan and I went deep-sea fishing there in…"

"Jordan, if you don't shut up about the t-shirt, you'll never get me out of it."

I took him by the hand and led him from the living room. The door to my bedroom was open and I'm sure he thought I was heading there. But there was another room he had to see first, the one across from mine. The door was ajar, the space lit by the glow from a *Hello Kitty* night-light. It was just bright enough to make out the crib and the tiny miracle swaddled in pink.

Jordan didn't move. I'm not even sure he was breathing. I know I wasn't. When panic struck, I started jabbering like a magpie. "She'll be three months old tomorrow, and I tell her every day how much we wanted her. She has your hair. She had those jet black curls when she was born, but her eyes are blue like mine. I know every parent thinks their child is beautiful but isn't she the most perfect thing you've ever seen? I named her Emily Theresa. We were hoping you'd provide the last name."

"You named her after my mother?" His voice barely recognizable, it sounded as if he were speaking from the bottom of a well.

"I figured it wouldn't hurt to be reminded of the kind of mother I want to be. Besides, it's a beautiful name."

"I had a right to know, Sydney."

"Yes, you did, but it was almost three months before it occurred to me to take a pregnancy test. I thought it was the stress of leaving you that was interfering with my period and making me sick. By then I wasn't sure you still wanted me and I couldn't risk that you'd take me back out of some misguided sense of honor. I swear I wasn't going to keep her from you,

Jordan. I want her to have what I never had, a real father to love her and protect her. We're booked to go back to the States in three weeks. I rented a small house in Paso Robles, so even if you don't want me anymore, you can see her whenever you want. I know you're angry but…"

Taking my arm, he pulled me from the nursery into the hallway and lowered his voice to a whisper. "Angry? I'm freaking furious you kept this from me and went through it alone, and I'm going to take it out of your hide, believe me. But right now, all I want to do is kiss my daughter good-night and fuck her mother senseless. And just so you know, she's the second most perfect thing I've ever seen."

Reaching up to touch his cheek, I knew my running days were over. "It's nice to know you're still the same smooth-talking devil I fell in love with."

"Yeah, well, this smooth-talking devil wants you naked on that bed in there. On second thought, put on those funky fuck-me shoes you were wearing earlier."

I rolled my eyes. "You can't be serious. I looked like *Boom-Boom Barbie*."

"What's your point?" He turned me toward the bedroom and smacked me on the butt. "The clock's ticking, Boom-Boom. You've got five minutes."

I made it in two.

EPILOGUE

If I'm honest I have to tell you I still read fairy-tales
and I like them best of all.
—Audrey Hepburn

Four days after the Prince of Darkness claimed his two fair maidens, we were back in California.

I barely had time to catch my breath and absorb the beauty of our new home before Emily and I were airborne again, destination Lake Tahoe. The flight was short, my anxiety off the charts. I knew that John and Emily would welcome their grand-daughter with open arms, but I was equally convinced they would never forgive me for my vanishing act. Jordan and Dylan thought my fears silly and did nothing to assuage them. Instead, while I was having a nervous breakdown at thirty thousand feet, they took turns blowing raspberries on Emily's belly. Men.

It seemed I had a lot to learn about family, the Dunhams in particular. For them, forgiveness was not so much a concept as a way of life; and as the beneficiary of their unconditional love, I was smothered in kisses and hugged till I squeaked.

With Lake Tahoe as a backdrop, our wedding took place at sunset in John and Emily's back yard. I had expected a family affair, perhaps a few friends and neighbors, but when John walked me down the rose-strewn aisle, close to fifty people were in attendance. Dropping her British reserve for the occasion, Grace competed with Amanda for the biggest cry-baby, both of whom confided they thought they'd never live to see me married.

The party was still going strong when Jordan and I kissed our precious girl good-night, left her grandmother with a list of unnecessary instructions and snuck off to our little A-frame in the woods where we *loved one another into oblivion and fucked like bunny rabbits.* Better late than never.

Our daughter is thriving. Clearly smitten with her daddy, she giggles whenever he walks in the room. The feeling is mutual. Attentive and loving, he's a wonderful father, everything and more I could have wished for my child.

Although I consult from time to time, the decision not to return to IIF was mine and I made it without hesitation. I prefer to work at home, to watch my daughter grow and channel my energy where it will do the most good. I still spend several hours a day working with the two missing persons' websites, but more often than not I'm facilitating an on-line support group for incest survivors. There are other on-line groups, good ones too, but with an estimated twenty million cases in the U.S. alone, we need all the help we can get. It was something Theresa wrote in one of her books that compelled me to take action, a phrase I'd chosen to ignore. She wrote that *secrets feed off the dark and the longer they stay hidden, the more power they assume.* How well I know.

Since I wasn't blessed with the best role model in the lower forty-eight, I'll confess that in the weeks following our marriage I searched the women's magazines for tips on how to be a wife. It was a sobering pursuit. According to the articles, with matrimony comes a dwindling of romance. Add a baby to the mix and passion has the shelf life of month-old milk. Now, almost a year later, I refer to them only when I need a good laugh.

Jordan is a wild man. Wickedly inventive, he's constantly devising new and clever ways to turn me on and deny me release, quite often at the most inappropriate times and places. Then there are the other times, quiet moments when Emily is sleeping and we're the only two people in the world. Our bodies entwined, we lie in bed and talk about everything, our day, our future and how lucky we are. Is it perfect? Close. It's a marriage after all, not a movie. I'm done with that.

He's also a planner by nature, so when he announced he was

taking care of the arrangements for our one-year anniversary, I knew it would be special.

My first clue that the day would be extraordinary was when a warm, wet tongue assaulted my ear instead of the dreaded alarm. I opened one eye enough to identify my assailant as Jordan and confirm the fact that I'd overslept. By a lot.

Groggy and naked, I bolted upright and shoved the hair from my face. "You turned off the alarm? Emily's probably..."

"Emily's fine. I bathed her, dressed her and we enjoyed a yummy repast of cereal and mashed bananas. Mike and Amanda already picked her up. They're spending the morning at the zoo and then dropping her off at Dylan's. He's taking her shopping and I think they're going to watch that new Disney film that's out on DVD. We'll pick her up at his place later tonight."

I scrambled to my knees. "Shopping? All she has to do is point at something and he buys it for her. I need a pith helmet and machete just to reach her bed."

"Relax. I told him if he bought her another stuffed toy, he was paying to have a wall knocked out."

"What did he say?"

"He signed a blank check." His large hands cradled my butt and he pulled me to him, nestling his erection in my tummy. "Now unless you want me to turn you around and have my way with this gorgeous ass, I suggest you haul it out of bed and into the shower."

I looped my arms around his neck and nipped his lower lip. "Wanna come?"

Lifting me to the floor, he propelled me to the bathroom. "Patience is its own reward, my girl, something we should probably work on today."

So it was going to be *that* kind of day. I draped my body against the doorjamb, a move I'd learned at *Naughty Nellie's*. "I thought an orgasm was its own reward. No, wait, I think it's virtue. Virtue is its own reward."

"Sydney!"

Despite my earlier misadventure, it was a perfect day. He'd planned everything down to the smallest detail, including a picnic lunch on Moonstone Beach. But the best part was when he made the turn-off to the cemetery, drove straight to Theresa's gravesite and laid a dozen red roses against her stone.

I knew he'd been there before and was thanking her for saving my life, but I also suspected there was more to it than that. Perhaps one day he'd tell me.

In the meantime, there was something I had to do, a final gesture to a friend I'd never met, one long overdue. At the edge of her headstone, I scooped out a hole and dropped in the locket.

I felt Jordan's hand on my shoulder. "You sure you want to do that?"

"It's time. You're giving me the best days of my life. I don't need a reminder of the worst."

He helped me to my feet and grazed my neck with the tips of his fingers. "Looks kind of bare. Guess I should replace it with something, huh?"

"Someday."

"How about now? Happy Anniversary, baby."

For once words failed me. It was the most amazing gift I'd ever received and the dearest, a platinum choker with a pendant set with pave diamonds, a hummingbird. "I can't...I don't..."

Laughing, he wrapped me in his arms. "Come on, sweetheart, let's go home. We'll put on *Benny and the Jets* and you can lay some more of those sexy moves on me." He leaned down and whispered, "If you're very good, I might even paddle your ass."

Whoopee. I giggled, inappropriately of course. "You wouldn't dare. I'm a wife and mother now."

"I'll be taking you over my knee when you're a grandmother. You love it."

"Do not."

"Do too."

"Brute."

"Brat."

So it came to pass. Having saved the damsels and slain the dragons, my handsome Prince whisked me to our castle, raised the drawbridge and took me to our bed.

And then he took me to the stars.

The end.

Author's Note

Domestic violence in the US has reached epidemic proportions with close to one-third of American women reporting physical or sexual abuse by a husband or boyfriend at some point in their lives. In households with children where domestic violence occurs, the children are abused 60 percent of the time.

There are ways we can help. If you know someone at risk, find a way to let her know help is out there or report the abuse. Since most women suffering at the hands of a violent spouse or partner arrive at shelters and safe houses with nothing more than their children in tow and the clothes on their backs, donations of money and clothing are gratefully accepted. We're in this together.

U.S. Hotline: 800.799.SAFE (7233)
Teen Dating Abuse Hotline: 866.331.9474

Peace, Shelby

AN EXCERPT FROM

Blessing

A WICKED TAILS STORY

COMING SOON

Nosy Parkers. I hated talking about myself. Right up there with crying, it made me feel weak and vulnerable. A soap opera wasn't an apt description. My life was a minefield, a misstep in any direction and it would blow up in my face.

With the shades closed against the morning sun, I slid down in the tub and let the hot, fragrant water work its magic. I was grateful for the solitude. It gave me a chance to remember and reflect on last night, the way they touched me, how my body responded. They'd been gentle, far more than I expected, their after-care tender and… practiced. They were Doms after all, experienced and skillful. Attempting to gain my trust, they were playing their parts, nothing more.

I washed my hair and used the hand-held sprayer to rinse it. When I wiped the water from my eyes, I almost plotzed. I wasn't sure what that meant but I'd heard Rene say it enough to know it could mean anything from throwing up to having a stroke. Sort of a one-size-fits-all word that suited the occasion perfectly. Jumping up, I backed against the wall.

Wearing much the same expression as he'd worn at the lagoon, Lucas stood beside the tub. Naked to the waist, his lower half covered in sweatpants, he stepped into the water and lifted me up. I felt lighter than air in his hands, as if I could float to the ceiling and beyond. "Wrap your legs around me, Abby."

Of course I did as he asked. Who wouldn't? Penning me between the wall and his chest, he rewarded me with a kiss.

His tongue went slow and deep, as if he had all the time in the world. He tasted like syrup, coffee and sin, three of my new favorite things.

I'm not certain who broke the kiss first but when I opened my eyes, his heated stare gave me the chills. "When was the last time you had a good cry?"

"Yesterday. I believe you were there, Sir."

"I'm not talking about the pain here." He squeezed my butt and laid his hand atop my left breast. "I'm talking about the pain here."

There was a fine line between nosy and no-fucking-way and he'd just tromped all over it. I shook my head. "You can't have that part of me. You can have anything but that."

His smile begged to differ. "We'll see."

Coming Soon

About the Author

A native of Southern California, Shelby is no stranger to the wonderful world of words. With the publication of her first story at the ripe old age of ten, she was hooked. Since then, she has enjoyed careers as a political speech writer and mainstream fiction author. Her worst job? Writing technical manuals for a large aerospace company. Her passion? Writing erotic romance. "The world is cold. Romance and great sex heat it up."

Shelby and her superhero husband are self-confessed vagabonds, moving whenever and wherever the spirit moves them, including a brief but happy stint on Vancouver Island, British Columbia. They currently reside in the Great American Southwest.

Visit Shelby at www.shelbykent-stewart.com.